MW01144391

# Tales from Under the Crevice

## By Zephyr Goza

The adventures continue at www.crevicetales.com

*The green people are under your sofa!*

*Zephyr Goza*

TALES FROM UNDER THE CREVICE ©2005 by
Zephyr Goza and L'eau Theque Productions
Published by L'eau Theque Productions

All the contents of this book are copyrighted 2004 by Zephyr Goza and
L'eau Theque Productions. No part of this book may be reproduced, stored in a
retrieval system, or transmitted in any form or by any means, electronic,
mechanical, recording, or otherwise, without prior written permission of Zephyr
Goza or L'eau Theque Productions.

You may send Zephyr adoring fan mail or bombs at:
Zephyr Goza
849 N. Hollywood Way #375
Burbank, CA
91505

There's still a lot of space left on this page, isn't there? I'd better fill it with
some important-looking stuff.

Tales From Under the Crevice ISBN: 1-4116-2001-1

Today's winning lottery numbers: 49, 87, 17, 908, 34.7762, 78, 56

Are you still reading this? Why? What's wrong with you? There's a whole
book to be read! Why are you wasting time reading the legal stuff? Get to the
story! Why are you addicted to fine print?

If you're still reading this, there may not be much hope. Since you
obviously have nothing better to do with your time, try sending a check for $200
made out to Zephyr Goza at the address above. Please don't send bombs. I was
just kidding about that. But the fan mail is OK.

*Dedicated to:*_____
*(Write your name here)*

# Chapter 1
# Crevice World

Okay, I know this is going to sound a little weird, but it's the truth: I don't have a house. Well, that's not entirely true. I do have one. But it's not the kind of house you're used to. My house is different. My house is a green conversion van. See? I told you it was a little unusual. It's an emerald colored 1995 Chevy towing a half-painted trailer full of props and costumes. The van has a New York license plate and the trailer is registered in Arkansas. Maybe someday, when the trailer is done being painted, you'll see my house on wheels. Maybe you're the guy who just drove by us on the freeway. Maybe, if you're walking along, you'll see our van parked there. If you ever read this, you would want to back away from the place where all this weird stuff happens. Or you would want to move closer and take a good look.

Anyway, as you might have guessed by the comment about the trailer, my family is a traveling theatre troupe, which often, most of the time, in fact, causes us to sleep in the van. My parents keep the back seat folded down for their bed, and I sleep on the floor. There are two other seats that are right against my parent's bed, so the overhanging area of the seat creates a sort of crevice or cubbyhole where my head goes, and this is where most of this stuff happened.

It was only the second night we'd owned the van, and I was thirteen years old, lying down to sleep on my Rugrats pillow. Yes, I'm now a fourteen-year-old-boy, and yes, I *still* have a Rugrats pillow. Deal with it. Anyway, I was lying down to sleep, and I heard an odd little noise. It was sort of like a spider moving around, whatever that sounds like, but more like a really big spider with two feet. The next thing I knew, a small pair of glowing red eyes peeked over my pillow at me. A small little man that accompanied the odd little footstep noise clambered over my pillow. Well, to say a man is an exaggeration. He was a male, to be certain, but he was not a man any more than a male squirrel would be a man. He was sort of like an elf, but with green skin and red eyes. He was about the size of my index finger.

I was a little surprised, since I am not used to odd little green people interrupting my sleep. The little creature seemed equally surprised to see me. He poked me curiously. Then he clambered onto my hand, carefully climbing up my arm. He stared at me a moment.

"Come with me," he grunted.

"Why?" I asked, sure I must be hallucinating.

"Just do it," he said. "Follow me." His voice was squeaky, like a cat singing with a rusty hinge.

Now, unlike kids in fantasy books, I am not likely to follow an odd little green person I have just met into who knows where, especially if he is two and a half inches tall, and is may fit into many places where I would get stuck. And I am even less likely to follow him if it is the middle of the night, and if I get stuck, I would just have to think, *oh, well*, and be satisfied to sleep wherever I am stuck. At least until morning, when somebody gets a saw and cuts me out, if I was ever discovered at all. I could be left there until I waste away into a skeleton, by which time I might be able to get through.

Fictional kids in fictional books seem to have no problem saying, "Oh, what a *very* lovely idea! I think I follow some green little elf I found in a crevice to who knows where, possibly find out he's a cannibal who's been starved for a month, or an illusion who will drive me crazy and make me burn everything I see, or a leprechaun who wants me to eat buckshot! Oh, this shall be a *wonderful* adventure!" This is why I am a real person and not a boy in some fantasy book. I'm sure it is a very hard occupation, and I quite like being a real person instead.

*This is not entirely true* So whenever a lie or half truth in this book is going to appear, I will warn you in italics, *like this*. I may use a few stretchers to present a more flattering image of myself. Other than that, this book is entirely true, to the best of my beliefs and abilities.

*This is a huge lie* I, being my bold, adventurous, handsome self, *this is true* I followed the elf *this is not* without further question or cause.

And as I squeezed in behind him, a most curious thing happened. The ground seemed to fall out from under me. A strange wind began blowing. And then, just as suddenly, it stopped. When I looked at the elf again, he was my size.

I started to say something, but the odd, no longer little elf wasn't listening. I hurried to keep up with him. We ran past some books crammed next to my pillow and ducked under a metal bar. Finally, as we approached the side of the van, the elf darted into a little crack, which was where the wall that my head was against stopped before the next wall began. I squeezed through.

Finally, we approached a plastic grating that led to the air conditioner. The elf crawled in, and I followed suit. "Be careful," the elf cautioned. "There's a drop..." *whoosh!* He disappeared. I took a step further, and *whoosh!* I disappeared too. Well, okay, so I didn't really disappear, or I wouldn't be here writing this.

What really happened was that I fell down a hole. A really, really big drop. I held my breath and bravely withstood it *that was a lie, I was screaming my head off.* I saw little creature's telltale glowing red eyes a long way off down the shaft. Then I started bumping against the walls. I slid down a wall for a very long time. Then the wall started to get bumpy. Very bumpy. The blackness started slowly fading away into a sky. Somewhere along the way, the other three walls of the shaft had disappeared. I looked down to see that the wall I had been sliding on had turned into what looked like the trunk of a palm tree, and I felt the unfamiliar sensation of falling from about eighty-seven stories.

It was a very long fall, to say the least. But when I hit the soft sand, it didn't hurt a bit. I was still dazed, though. I looked all the way up to the top of the palm tree, which had to be about three-quarters of a mile high, if not higher. At the top was a mass of red palm leaves, about the size of a cloud.

I just lay there in the soft sand a little while and stared up. Then I sat up and began to gather my surroundings. I was on an island. The green creature sat next to me. He looked around. Just about sixty feet away was more land, but this time in the form of a forest or jungle.

"You," I said. "Who are you? What are you? An elf?"

"Most certainly not," he replied. "I am a gremlin! And my name is Serrin. You are a human, are you not?"

"I am."

"Then follow me just a little farther and we shall come to my village."

Serrin casually walked into the water. He looked back and saw I was not following. "What's the matter?" He asked.

"Uh…" I said. "I'm in my pajamas. I can't get these wet."

"Don't worry! The water here isn't wet."

"How can you have water that's not wet? And if that is true, then how do you know what wet is?"

"I don't know! It's just…some parts of it are wet. Others aren't."

"Oh, *that* makes sense. How do you tell?"

"Wet is blue. Dry is green."

I had absolutely no reason to trust Serrin.

But for some reason I did. I trusted him just enough to dip my foot into the green water. Oddly enough, he was right. It wasn't wet. So I ventured all the way in. It was a weird experience. The water was cold and damp, just damp enough that I could feel it, but not enough to make my clothes wet.

We waded through the water until we reached the other side, which took about a minute. When we got to the other side, I took a good look back to the top of the palm tree, now outlined by a rising sun, which I thought was weird, since the last time I had checked, it was nighttime. Anyway, the top of the palm tree was a mass of red.

I followed Serrin through several layers of jungle until we reached a village, consisting of a mass of huts made of bamboo and topped with hay. People were coming out of their huts and staring at me.

Sorry, gremlins, not people. They all resembled Serrin, though of course there were males and females with different body builds and hair colors and styles.

One of these gremlins approached Serrin with a quirky walk, using half-lopsided motions. He had a head of blue hair tied in a short queue down his back. He had heavy bangs. "Hey, Serrin!"

"What?"

"You got one?"

"Oy, Ragnark, o' course I got one!"

"Well, sorry, I just…" he half hobbled, half pranced after us to catch up. "…never seen one before."

Here I interjected curiously. "Uh…are you another gremlin?"

"Of course he is!" said Serrin.

"Of course I'm not!" said Ragnark. "I'm a goblin. Has Serrin been spouting that gremlin nonsense again?"

"Quiet, Ragnark! You're a gremlin and you know it."

The conversation carried on like this for quite some time. Finally, a third thing joined us as we approached a stone temple with strange writing on the wall. "Are you a goblin or a gremlin?" I asked reluctantly.

"Neither! I am an elf!"

By now I was getting terribly confused. They all looked exactly alike. "Oh, hi, Bednik."

We walked directly to the wall of the temple. Serrin pointed to the writing on the wall. "See that?" he said. "That's our village laws. Right there it says that each night one of us has to go searching for humans in the next world, and if we find one, to bring 'em here."

"Oh." I was afraid the next part was going to involve a blood sacrifice. Fearfully, I asked, "And then?"

"Uh..." Serrin looked a little embarrassed. "I, um, don't know. That's as far as we've been able to translate it."

"So...you brought me here for nothing because of an ancient village law written in some language you don't understand."

"Well, actually, it's just the second part we don't understand."

"How do you know that the whole thing doesn't just say that chucking stones at squirrels is fun?"

Here Bednik popped in. "He has a point, Serrin. Except that chucking stones at squirrels isn't as amusing as you'd think."

Serrin glared at him. "I translated it. Sort of. It's just that I don't know all the characters yet. I don't see anybody else even *trying.*"

Ragnark lit up. "Who says we brought him here for nothing, eh? To the pub!"

The crowd that had gathered around to stare at me went wild! I was dragged away into the stampede by Serrin, Ragnark, and Bednik.

# Chapter 2
# The Story

The pub was a bamboo building with a thatch roof and two torches outlining the entrance. The windows were made of a blurry glass with iron bars supporting them. Inside was a long wooden table with straw woven stools.

Here I was introduced to a thick, delicious drink called slurk. We sat in the pub all day drinking slurk and telling stories. I had many stories to tell, all of which they were quite interested in.

Eventually, night fell, and the pub closed. We gathered around a huge bonfire, talking and laughing. Finally, someone shouted, "Hey, Serrin! Tell the story of Ranook and the Cursed Ones!" The circle fell silent.

"Nay! Do ye want to bring 'em down on us in a flash? Silence, you!" hissed Serrin. A brief glance passed between Bednik and Ragnark. "The last time the story was told, there were sounds all through the night! Inhuman sounds. And two of the guard went missing."

"We're right by the Galian folk! What could happen?" protested the bystander.

"And we've got you and the guard to protect us!" shouted an attractive (by elf standards) female from the crowd.

"Well," sighed Serrin reluctantly. "I guess you have a point there." He cocked his head back and took a long sip of slurk. "All right. It began many years ago on a stormy night."

"Ranook was a demon of a child. He was sharp and strong, and always getting into trouble. He always got what he wanted, and fought with anyone who stood in his way."

"Then one day, his parents got killed. Brutally. Ranook went insane. He sought the power of something called…the Bloodlust Stone." Here the crowd let out a collective gasp. They were really getting into it.

"This stone," continued Serrin, "if held by one pure of heart and of good morals, can only be used for good. But Ranook was not one of these people. His heart was twisted with vengeance. The stone transformed him into a creature of pure evil. He found the people who had killed his parents and trapped their souls in the stone. They became his servants. Empty husks. He has gone on trapping people like this, committing them to his will. And that is the story of Ranook and the Cursed Ones."

The circle burst into applause, cheering and hollering. Then the lightning started. Thunder flashed. Rain began and wind started howling. A bolt of lightning flashed towards us, stopping several feet from Serrin's chest, as though pointing an accusing finger at him.

Everyone turned tail and ran, save for Serrin and myself. Serrin stared at the sky, speechless. Two dark red spots ran across the sky, as though they were soulless eyes staring us down.

But it took more than that to take down two tough old dogs like us. An inhuman screech raced across the sky. That was plenty to take down two tough old dogs like us. We ran for our lives to Serrin's tent, where we sat quaking for the next couple of hours.

Finally I managed to speak. "Serrin," I said.

"Aye?"

"Is that tale true?"

"I hope not." he whispered.

The next morning was cold and gray. Fog was in everywhere. The village was silent. Yet through the fog I heard a sound. A distant sound, some sort of melody, the notes sweet yet eerie. "What's that?" I asked Serrin. "Oh," he said. "That'll be the Galians. They sing like this every morning. They live up in the tree."

"You mean the big one."

"Of course! What else would I mean?"

"Any number of the thousands of trees around us"

"Well, that's beside the point here."

"Not really."

"Oh, shut up." I could tell he was still troubled by last night's events.

I could recall something being said about the Galians. That they were supposed to protect us. "Why are the Galians supposed to protect us?" I asked.

"The Galians," he said, "are really a gentle and peaceful folk. But when provoked, they are fearsome fighters. They have a strong sense of honor and justice."

"Well, then," I said, "we're not in any real danger are we?"

He glanced at me skeptically. "We'll see."

I found myself staring up into the sun. The large palm tree with the red top extended almost a mile above me. Serrin opened his knapsack and pulled out two bamboo rockets. "Why are we here again?" I asked.

"Requesting help," he said. He tied the tops of the fuses together and set the rockets down some distance away from me. Retrieving two flint rocks from his knapsack, he struck them together, sparking the fuses. He ran away from the rockets to stand beside me. We watched as the fuses burned down.

Then, with a loud BOOM, the rockets took off. We watched as they moved away into the sky.

Several minutes later, something fell towards us. It was a rope. "Here we go," said Serrin. "Hold on. Tight!" I did. In another second, we were flying upwards. I saw a huge boulder whiz past me on the way up.

At last we landed on a wooden platform at the top. Two strange creatures helped us up. They looked almost human, save for their lizard-like eyes and skin. They were muscular but still maintained a peaceful appearance. I leaned over the railing. Big mistake. I was about a mile up, and swaying uncertainly in the breeze. Down below I could see the boulder as a tiny dot dropping into the sand. I looked up and the rope and pulley system above me.

"Hail, Serrin," hissed one of the Galians.

"Hail." Replied Serrin, saluting.

"Whom do you seek?" asked the other Galian.

"Head Councilman."

"Aye," was the stiff response.

The two Galians led us off the platform. I was amazed. The Galians had literally built a community up here. We were led through swaying suspension bridges; through planks and turrets. There were paths leading into a spider web maze of bridges and ropes.

Finally we arrived at a wooden building three stories tall. We entered and climbed up a spiral staircase.

Coming out on the roof of the building we saw the head councilman sitting on the throne.

He was as slim and muscular as the others, wearing a simple red robe that was as tattered as everyone's clothes. He was young still, maybe in his twenties and his black hair was tied back in a queue that extended halfway down his back. He wore three earrings on his right ear.

Serrin knelt before him. He grunted. "Dispense with the formalities, Serrin. You know me well enough. Why are you here?" asked the councilman. He glanced at me a moment, then added, "And who is this odd creature?"

Serrin remained on his knees. "He is a human. From another world."

"A human!" He got up and inspected me curiously. "I'd heard stories about your kind. Never seen one though."

"Well," I said "Here I am."

"Your clothes . . . aren't they uncomfortable?"

"Oh, my PJs . . . well, they're not for climbing in."

"Naram!" he yelled. One of the others glanced over. "Bring him some Galian clothing." Naram nodded. I saw him depart by grabbling a rope and swinging off the roof.

The councilman noticed that Serrin was still kneeling. "Why do you still kneel?"

"Because," said Serrin. "I have a huge favor to ask."

"Then it will be denied unless you stand." Serrin stood.

"We required your help, your protection."

"Against whom?"

"Erm . . .against . . .Ranook?" The councilman started.

"You have angered Ranook? My friend, that is an evil against which there is no protection."

"I was afraid you'd say that."

"But we will do our best." Serrin was elated.

This whole conversation was very interesting, but there was something that interested me even more. It was a dark mass moving through the fog way off in the distance. "Can I borrow a telescope?" I asked. The head councilman threw me his telescope. I looked through it towards the gray-black mass. It was people. Millions of them. Except it didn't look like people. Their colors were all wrong, making them look more like skeletons than people. I handed the telescope to the head councilman.

"It would appear that you really have angered Ranook." He said. "I would recommend that you evacuate immediately."

"Aye. You stay here...whatever your name is."

"Zephyr."

"Right. Zephyr. You stay here. I have to go evacuate the village." Serrin left, but he left in style— by jumping off the roof. I started after him. "Don't." said the councilman.

"But..."

"Don't worry about it. It doesn't hurt on this sand, remember?" Recalling the fall I had experienced as I first entered this world, I stopped.

"Does it never hurt to fall in this world?"

"No. This sand is the only place where you will not sustain damage." I nodded. "But enough of that. Do you know how to wield a sword?"

"Uh...no."

"Then you shall learn."

As he led me away to change into my new clothes, I was becoming less and less sure I wanted to stay here.

"Wait," I said. "I don't remember volunteering to fight."

"We need you to fight with us. We need all the manpower we can get. I'll make it up to you later."

"Um…I'd like my bed right about now."

Ignoring me, he grabbed a rope tied to a pole on the opposite side of the roof. He waited there a moment. "Are you coming?" he said. I finally realized he meant for me to follow him. I suddenly wished I hadn't followed Serrin into the crevice. Seeing that I had no other options, I shrugged and managed to mumble "Sure." I walked over to him and grabbed the rope. Tightly. After my first experience with flying onto the platform, I was ready for anything.

"Here we go," he said, untying the rope. "Hold on." He leapt from the platform, dragging me with him into a mass of red palm leaves. *Wham!* The full force of the swing hit me as the leaves blurred by. It was like a steep drop on a roller coaster. My insides floated inside me. I was just thankful that they were not floating *outside* me. It's not the most pleasant experience, but plenty of us, including myself, put ourselves through it on a regular basis for no good reason.

We swung onto a path and I collapsed in a heap. It was then that I realized that in this village, you don't go anywhere unless you do it in style. He helped me up and took me into a bamboo building marked *Armory*. I was amazed. A long row of neatly organized swords lay on the table. On the opposite wall hung dozens of swords and bows. The head councilman gestured to the table. "Those swords belong to our warriors However, you may choose a weapon from this wall." I glanced over the huge selection. There were various swords and bows as well as spears, battle axes, crossbows, clubs, spikes, shuriken, and shields of all sizes and shapes.

However, there was one weapon that seemed to call me. It was a long sword, the stone hilt ending in the shape of an intricately detailed lion's head. It looked like it hadn't been used in centuries. I unhooked it from the wall.

"This one," I said. "This is it."

"You're sure?" He looked at me in puzzlement.

"Yeah. This is it." He lifted the weapon from me and, muttering some sort of mumbo-jumbo, placed it on the table. He nodded slowly.

"Zephyr," he said slowly. "There may be more to you than meets the eye."

"Mister...Head Councilman...sir..."

"Please, call me Morn."

"Morn. What did you mean by that?"

He just shook his head and led me into the next room. There we bumped into Naram, carrying a fresh set of Galian clothes. He tossed them to me. "These are yours." He said.

"Excellent," said Morn. He gestured to a room covered by a curtain. "You may change in there." I stepped into the rather nondescript room. It was three bamboo walls and the curtain. A mirror adorned one wall. I unfolded the clothes.

When I had finished changing, I wore a white shirt with a V-shaped cut hanging down just past my chest. A loose pair of tan pants hung on my legs. The pants tucked into a pair of boots that extended almost to my knees. I wore a red belt made of a simple cloth. Two leather arm braces clung to the lower half of my arm.

I stepped out to face Naram and Morn. "Wonderful," said Morn. "Now we'll put you to work." I started to panic.

"Work? I don't want to work!"

"Don't worry," said Naram. "It'll be easy."

It was almost twilight now. The sun painted pink hues against the sky. They led me back to the platform I had first come up on. There were two large boulders resting on the platform. Two tough looking

Galian men shoved the boulders over the side. The boulders set off the rope and pulley system. A moment later, Serrin and Bednik were hoisted onto the platform.

Bednik, with his quick, graceful motions, glided over to me. I saw glittering lights off in the distance. "Morn!" I yelled.

"You address the Head Councilman by name? There are few of us who are allowed to do that." Morn joined us.

"What do you need?" he asked.

"Your telescope." He handed it to me. Looking through the eyepiece, I focused on the glittering light. It was Ranook's undead men. They held torches. Then I realized it wasn't just men. There were women too. Their gray, clammy skin could be seen through their tattered dresses and work clothes. And then I saw something that made me really mad. It was the children. Children of all ages and sizes had been captured in Ranook's deadly trap.

My blood boiling, I handed the telescope to Bednik. He peered through it. "It's Ranook's undead," he offered, controlling his emotion. "They carry torches."

"Torches?!" Shouted Morn in surprise. "They are undead! They know their way in perfect dark! Why do they need torches?" Suddenly it came to me.

"Torches are fire. Fire burns wood. The village is wood."

"They plan to burn the Village of Panok!" exclaimed Bednik.

# Chapter 3
# Evacuation

Hearing our shouting, Serrin rushed over.

"Then we must warn the other villages!"

"What other villages are there?" I asked.

"The fairy village," offered Serrin. "Crescent Moon."

"There is another elf village…" started Bednik.

"Gremlin!" yelled Serrin.

"Elf!"

"Gremlin!"

"Elf!"

"Gremlin!"

"Little green things who can't decide what they are which is unimportant under the current circumstances anyway!" I yelled.

"That about settles it." said Morn.

"Very well, then," said Bednik. "There is another village of the little green things who can't decide what they are which is unimportant under the current circumstances anyway. It is called Shanar, and it is just beyond the fairy village."

"I'm sure little green things who can't decide what they are which is unimportant under the current circumstances anyway of Shanar would be…"

Cutting Serrin off, I said, "Um…could we maybe abbreviate that to…say…" I pulled a name off the top of my head. "Glunches?"

"Glunches, fine. I'm sure the Glunches of Shanar would be willing to help us out on this." Finished Serrin.

"I think we should gather them into our army. Gather as large a force as possible." said Bednik.

"No," Morn replied. "Up here is the best vantage point. We can see the movement of their troops. We're out of reach from arrows. We can send a few scouts to warn the others." That sounded like good reasoning to me, so I left well enough alone. Morn left to get some scouts to send to the other villages.

The two Galians had finished hauling the boulders back up. They waited as something was tied to the ropes down below. Then they shoved the boulders off the platform. A moment later, Ragnark flew up, standing on top of a large stone slab with writing on it.

"Oh, good, it's safe." said Serrin. Upon closer inspection, the strange writing clearly identified it as the temple's wall. My eyes bulged. They began hauling it onto the platform. "You took apart the temple?" It was more a statement of disbelief that I uttered instead of any sort of question. Serrin coughed uncomfortably.

"Dismantled," he corrected. "Dismantled temporarily." Ragnark hobbled over to the head councilman.

"The provisions and warriors are coming up now," he said. "The villagers will be up shortly." Morn nodded. Having been acknowledged, Ragnark then proceeded to watch the movements of Ranook's army with undue interest.

I was going to make conversation with Ragnark, but I was dragged away by Morn, who needed my help loading Panok's supplies into the supply bay.

We stacked the boxes neatly in pyramids in large, dusty supply rooms. Our bodies and minds were concentrated on the task at hand, but there was always a nagging sensation at the back of our minds that reminded us that Ranook's troops were drawing ever closer.

By the time the villagers started coming up, it was dark. The torches that illuminated Ranook's army had drawn dangerously close.

A chill began to blow with the wind, sending a shiver down my spine. Then the gong sounded. "Call to arms!" I heard someone yell. I rushed to the armory, grabbing my sword. A few people looked at me strangely as I clipped it to my belt.

I spotted Bednik at the wall full of weapons. He glanced over them until he found a pair of battleaxes that suited him nicely. He gave them a couple of practice swings. I managed to make my way over to him. He glance at my sword in surprise.

"Oh, enough already!" I shouted. "What is so interesting about the sword?"

Everyone looked at me in surprise because of my sudden outburst. Embarrassed, Bednik and I pretended to look around for the culprit as well. When everyone resumed their business, Bednik said, "It's just that the sword you wear belonged to Panok, the founder of our village. He's the one who chiseled out the letters on the temple wall. Or at least that's what Serrin says."

"So? What's so special about that?"

"Nobody until now had even been able to hold that sword. It's been cast in a spell so strong it feels like it weighs a ton."

"Morn had no problem holding it."

"Of course not. He's one of the few able to cast an anti-gravity spell long enough to hold it for just a few seconds. Even he can't draw the sword. We're all just surprised that you can even hold it."

Just out of curiosity, I tried drawing the sword. It came out of the sheath easily, fitting snugly in my hand. I held it up to the light. Its blade was blue, glittering and sparkling as I tilted it back and forth in the light. Some of the Galians in the armory stared with their jaws dropping. Others took discreet glances. Just about everyone was looking at me in one way or another. I quickly sheathed it to avoid all the extra attention.

"I don't get it," I said. "Why is there a spell to make it heavy?"

"No," he said, shaking his head. ""Heaviness is just a side effect. The spell is something different. This sword is the only one that can destroy an undead."

I clipped the sword to my belt, at last understanding some of this. I was going to make further conversation, but I smelled smoke outside. Rushing outside with everyone else, I saw the village on fire a mile below, the smoke rising in thick plumes up into the sky.

Finding Serrin, I knelt beside him. He wore a bow on his back and a quiver full of arrows. His glowing red eyes darted nervously around, scanning the action on the village below. His eyes momentarily flashed yellow in anger. Then he noticed me. Or, more importantly, the sword at my side. Trying to cover his surprise, he tossed me a bag. It was brown leather, looking old and unused. It was about the size of a pebble.

"Don't open it unless you're in a real pinch," said Serrin. "It may help you out, but it can only be used once, so don't open it unless we have a real emergency."

Neither of us noticed Morn approaching. "We may have an emergency now," he said. "Take a look." He handed me his telescope. Peeking through it, I saw something I would rather not have. Axes. They were carrying axes. Not even able to speak, I handed the telescope to Serrin, who looked through it without too much interest. "So?" he said. "When chopped with an axe, the tree will replenish itself. Why worry?"

"Yes, that's true," explained Morn. "As long as the tree's roots have an ample supply of water. It's been living on the same underground supply of water for almost six hundred years. Water leaks in from the river, but it may not be enough."

"What are we going to do about it?" I inquired.

"Nothing, right now." Was the reply. "There's nothing we can do. We're going to retire half our soldiers. You two, Bednik and Ragnark are among them. We'll wake you at midnight and you'll take the watch."

I was tired enough, so that sounded like a good plan to me. Morn led us down a couple of paths until we reached a two story house supported by ropes.

"These ladies volunteered the only spare residence we had," said Morn. "You will be sleeping upstairs."

It should have struck me to leave immediately when he said "ladies", but cut me some slack. I was tired. We ventured one by one across the plank into the house, where we met Ragnark and Bednik, who had just arrived.

The four of us, seeing that no one else was around, ventured upstairs. That was where they ambushed us. Ten or fifteen young Galian women jumped out from every nook and cranny. They surrounded us in a matter of seconds. I had my sword halfway out before I realized what I was doing and put it back.

It's not that they were unattractive. Their skin was smooth, their eyes were hypnotizing, and their cheekbones pulled up high. They had sharp and elongated jaws.

Somehow, they split us up into two separate groups…Ragnark and I lost sight of Bednik and Serrin. We backed off into another room. The girls started to flood in after us. Ragnark grabbed a table and flipped it against the open doorway. I quickly caught on and stacked a chair on top of it. Before long, the room had no furniture and we had a barricade.

"How do we get out of this one?" I shouted. Ragnark grinned and pointed to the open window. "No way!" I responded.

"That's out only bet!" he said. The barricade was being slowly pushed in. I ran to the window and peered out. There were plenty of footholds.

"You first!" I yelled. He hoisted himself onto the windowsill and out the window. When he was a safe distance away, I followed suit. Holding on to the boards on the side of the house, I heard our barricade being smashed in. Not wanting to give away our location, I scrambled over to Ragnark before whispering, "Now what?"

Trying to whisper over the shrieks and giggles coming from inside, he said, "Now let's climb around the back and help out Bednik and Serrin."

If you ever have the opportunity to climb outside a wooden two-story house swaying back and forth a mile above the ground with undead skeletons patrolling below, I suggest you decline it.

We finally reached the other side of the house. We randomly peeked in windows until we was the remainder of the girls gathered around the fireplace. We jumped onto the roof and peered down the chimney. I could see the glowing eyes of Serrin and Bednik. They were trying to hold the fireplace doors shut and having a hard time of it. "Will the house fall if I cut one of these ropes?" I asked.

"Not likely, " said Ragnark. "Most of them are extras." I picked out the nearest rope.

"How about that one?" I pointed to it.

"Go ahead. " he shrugged. I jumped onto the rope and clambered to the end. Where it was tied to a palm leaf. I sliced the rope and came swinging to the side of the house. I used the rope to climb back to the roof and sheathed my sword. Then I dropped the rope down the chimney. "Climb up!" I yelled.

Serrin was the first to make his way out of the narrow chimney and was immediately followed by Bednik. Seeing the females start to climb the rope, Bednik used his axes to slice the rope in two, so it wouldn't support their weight.

Now, some of the houses were simple cubes, but this one had an angled triangular roof. We quickly discovered a place where the weather had eaten a hole in the roof and we climbed in. It was pitch black inside the little crawl space and Bednik and Ragnark quickly fell asleep. It was dry and warm in there, but old and musty. In any case, it was better than being surrounded by a gang of gabbing, giggling Galian girls. Boy that was fun to write.

I almost fell asleep, but there was something still bothering me. "Serrin?" I whispered.

"Hmm?"

"What about my world?"
"What about it?"

"Well … I need to go back. I've already been gone too long. People will miss me."

"No," he said. "According to Panok's early experiments, a day equals five minutes in your world."

29

Satisfied, I fell asleep.

# Chapter 4
# Dragons

The next morning found us on top of the roof sparring with our weapons. My sword moved with ease, as though it was telling me where to move and what to do.

We were up there fighting when we wondered why Morn hadn't come to wake us. Just as I voiced the question out loud, Morn came running up the plank towards the house. "What're you doing up there?" he yelled.

We made our way down from the roof. "Why didn't you wake us last night?" I asked.

"I came to," he said. "But the occupants of the house said something about using a magical disappearing spell and flying up the fireplace chimney."

"Nonsense." said Bednik.

"That's what I said," said Morn. "But we have an emergency right now."

"What is it?" asked Ragnark.

"Come see for yourself."

We were led down the plank and through a series of pathways until we were back at the platform. We groaned in distress. The undead were climbing up the side of the tree . They were only about a quarter of the way up. Frantic archers shot arrows with all their might. The undead would just get right back up again.

"Now what?" I moaned. An explosion sounded in the sky. I ducked and drew my sword, twirling it around in search of the enemy. Bright colors screamed across the sky.

Then all was silent. The head councilman grinned. "We are not without our allies."

"What was that?" I sheathed my sword.

"A signal."

"To whom?" He just shook his head. A moment later, something appeared on the horizon. It was like a huge, dark cloud. Upon closer inspection, I could see it was actually amass of tiny dots. As they drew closer, I could make out what appeared to be wings. They drew closer still. They were approaching at a rapid pace until I could make out various colors and patterns. Before I knew what was happening, I found myself face to face with one. It was huge . It was brown with yellow stripes, rearing a head that easily reminded one of a T. Rex. Its forked tongue flicked in and out, tasted the air around it. Its wings stretched against the sky as it settled with its huge velociraptor-like claws onto the handrail. It flicked its tail around like a mace. I was face to face with a dragon.

"Is that a dragon?" I asked nervously.

"Yes." said Serrin. It hissed at him.

"No," corrected Morn. "It is a terrawumquazzalarnerapheliusdorimino'sa. But for lack of a better word, you may call it a dragon." It reared up proudly at being introduced correctly. They started loading the villagers onto the dragons. They flew away with either three villagers or a load of supplies on their back. "Where are we going?" I asked.

"First, to gather allies and supplies," said Morn. "Then we'll have to try to escape."

"Spend the rest of lives running?" asked Serrin.

"Until we think of a better plan."

"I need to learn when not to tell a story."

The dragons came faster and faster, with more and more people piling onto them. Suddenly I realized that I would have to ride on one of these. "Do I actually have to ride a terrawhatsit?" I fearfully inquired.

"Yes." said Morn rather bluntly. "Ah, good, the scout's arrived." a dragon flew up with a scout on it. "Well?" asked Morn. "What's the word?"

"It doesn't look good." the scout replied. "The fairy village is silent as a grave. I heard something massive moving through the underbrush, so I got out of there fast. Something else cut me off before I managed to reach the village of Shanar. I didn't get a good look at it …" he patted the dragon playfully. "…She destroyed it, whatever it was. Turns out they were foraging in the area."

"So that's how they responded to the distress signal so fast." said Morn.

Then someone dragged me, Serrin and Ragnark onto a dragon and we were off. It was an exhilarating ride. First it was a free fall towards the ground, then our dragon barrel rolled in midair. He thought it was amusing. We did not. We ducked back into loops and twirls until our dragon tired of it and settled for straight flying.

The landscape was flowing below us. The trees gave way to flat plains and rolling hills, and then into trees again. We spiraled down to join a flock of dragons and villagers in a small clearing.

Dismounting from the terrawumquazzalarnera-pheliusdorimino'sa, I could barely make out the tall palm tree on the horizon.

I took a good look at my surroundings. At first glance it appeared to be just a normal clearing. Upon closer inspection, I could make out small buildings on the ground. They were little, multicolored mounds with doors and windows. Then I noticed the little doorways in the tree trunks. And the houses way up in the treetops. I guessed that this was the fairy village. Nobody budged or dared to speak.

Taking soft steps, making as little noise as possible, I set about exploring the area. I pushed through leaves and vines. As I pushed one bush aside, I gave a sudden yell that caused everyone to turn and stare. I had just uncovered the body of a female fairy. She was only about the size of my finger, even in the shrunken state I was in. She wore what appeared to be an outfit consisting entirely of leaves. Tiny leaves, big enough to wrap around her body, but no bigger. Her silvery-blonde hair had been done up in a bun, but now hung in wisps about her shoulders. Her eyes were closed as though asleep, her mouth slightly open, as though in a whisper. She had wings that were almost the size of her body. But none of this was her most distinguishing feature. No, her most distinguishing feature was that she was cut in half, with some sort of purple liquid oozing out around her abdomen. I looked away and almost threw up.

# Chapter 5
# The Fairies

Serrin had been attracted by my shout and was looking the body over. "Curious," said Serrin. "This is not the work of the undead."

"Why not?" I muttered, my hands over my mouth.

"Well, a fairy is one of the few whose soul cannot be captured," Serrin explained. "So some undead might have killed them in frustration but the undead are not this graceful and would not hide the bodies. In addition, it is very hard to surprise a fairy and if the undead had managed to do it, there would be tracks and evidence everywhere." He was right. Everything was still.

We gathered up the bodies for a mass funeral. The bodies piled higher and higher, but I was still staring at the fairy I had discovered. She had been moved to the ground. A pair of Galians inspected the cut. One of them whispered something in Morn's ear as he dismounted from his dragon.

"Too bad we don't know the spell," said Ragnark. I hadn't even realized he was standing next to me.

"What spell?" I asked.

"There's a life spell," he sighed. "It's specifically formulated to bring fairies back to life, but none of our bunch knows what it is."

"Well, that should be our next step then!" I said. "Let's figure out the spell!"

He shook his head. "The spell is probably quite complex. It would slow us down to figure it out. The key to figuring it out is hundreds of miles away. Trying to figure out the spell would put us in greater danger of Ranook's troops. The spell must be performed within six hours of the fairy's death anyway, and by the looks of things, it's been at least three hours since this happened." Ragnark left.

I just sat down next to the female fairy. The whole thing reminded me oddly of a scene from Peter Pan, so for some reason, I muttered to myself, "I do believe in fairies."

When I glanced down at the female fairy, she didn't seem to be cut in half. I blinked. Some color was coming back into her cheeks. Her lips were moving! She fluttered her wings, then sat up slowly. She looked around and took stock of her surroundings. "Who released me from the bonds of death?" her voice had a ringing quality to it—it's hard to describe. Her eyes settled on me. "Was it you who spoke the words?"

"Well, I, uh…I mean…I wouldn't know. Well, I…unless…er…wait a minute…what're the…the, um…it's…is it…you mean…I do believe in fairies?" (Impressive speech, huh?) Another one sat up. A male this time.

"Those are the words," she said coolly, eyeing me. "But how did you learn them?"

"I…uh…"

"You must be a sorcerer of high power!"

"Not really. I'm just a human."

"How did you learn the spell?"

"I…guessed it. Blind luck…" she seemed to not quite believe my words.

By now I had definitely attracted some attention. People were staring at me from all directions. Morn hurried over. "Did this boy revive you?" he asked the two fairies.

"Yes." replied the male. His voice sounded like a young child's. Then I realized that he was a young child. His hair was blond on top with dark sideburns running down his temple. He was stretching his wings.

"I do believe in fairies!" I blurted out. A fairy whose head had been hacked off had his head fly back on. He sat up.

"Fool!" hissed the female fairy. "Must you let everyone hear the words?" I ignored her.

"I do believe in fairies! I do believe in fairies! I do believe in fairies! I do believe in fairies! I do believe in fairies!" Fairy after fairy was flying together into a bright, glittering ball.

The fairy had realized that it was too late to stop me. She sat back with her hands over her face.

The whole scene must have looked quite amusing, really. I was running around the whole clearing like an idiot with my hands over my head, yelling "I do believe in fairies!" as loud as I could. Everyone was staring at me, and the fairies were all flitting around in confusion, having broken up the big sphere. Ragnark was grinning over by a tree. He was the only one who looked just mildly surprised. Nothing seemed to phase him.

I kept running until I bumped into one of the dragons. It sent the sack that Serrin had given me flying into the air. I rushed to retrieve it. The female fairy caught it first. She dropped it quickly, as though some invisible force had burned her hand. I snatched it up. She stared at me a moment, trying to recover. Then, trying to cover up her reaction, she glanced away. I was tempted to open the bag and look inside, but in the end I decided to heed Serrin's advice.

It was then that I noticed Morn staring at me with one eyebrow raised. "If you are done making your magic now," he said. "I have an announcement to make, one that I'm sure your fairy friend will verify. According to our studies, the fairy folk were not attacked by Ranook's undead. They were attacked by a tribe of Nariss."

"That's what I thought." muttered Serrin.

Several people gasped. I also gasped (for dramatic effect). Then, after a pause, I asked, "Who or what are the Nariss?"

"Don't ask." shuddered Morn.

"Why not join forces with them?" asked someone in the crowd. This provoked a lot of excitement.

"Who said that?" shouted Morn in rage. "Step forward!" Ragnark calmly hobbled out from the crowd, leaning on a stick he had found.

"I said," he coolly continued, as though nobody had heard him. "Why not join forces with them?"

"You are mad to suggest such an idea!" yelled Morn.

"Am I?" shrugged Ragnark. "With such a powerful wizard on our side…" he winked at me. "…indisputably proven by the fact that he rose all the fairies from death…they would likely comply. Plus, Ranook is a threat to them, too. If we gather a large enough army, we could stand a fighting chance."

"I-Impossible!" blustered the fairy. "He would be required to prove it." Ragnark gave her a good once-over.

"She looks like proof to me."

"And so do they." said Morn, gesturing to all the other fairies. "If it's either get killed by the Nariss or get killed by Ranook, let's deprive Ranook of the pleasure."

"You can't be serious!" the fairy yelled. "There's no way that would work!"

"Only one way to find out." replied Ragnark.

"You won't be having us come along." said the fairy. Serrin was tapping my shoulder, indicating that he wanted to whisper something in my ear.

"Tell her," he whispered. "That as your first favor, you demand that she comes with us." I had no idea what that meant. "And tell her she must order her tribe to come with her."

I took a deep breath and loudly cleared my throat. She whirled on me. "What do you want?" she hissed.

"As my first favor," I said. "I demand that you come with us and order your tribe to follow." She went chalk white. I thought for a moment that she might fall out of the air, but she collected herself.

"Let us gather our things." she said quietly, and fluttered off.

"What did I just do?" I asked Serrin. He grinned.

"The five fairy favors. There's a rule about resurrecting fairies: the fairy owes whoever revived them five favors."

"You mean I have a whole village of fairies who each owe me five favors?" he nodded enthusiastically. "Wow," I said. "That's quite a deal."

"The only thing you can't ask of them is more favors. Five's the limit."

The fairies took a short time packing. We were off in a matter of minutes. I led the way with the female fairy guiding me. We conversed a great deal during this time, and I learned that her name was Mystique.

We worked our way deeper and deeper into the forest. At last we found our way to a place where the trees thinned out a little. The ground was soft and moist. At last we found a small clearing with small mounds rising from the ground. Steam rose from the mounds. "This is it." announced Mystique. "You first." I stared at the hole in one of the mounds.

"I don't get it. What do I do?"

"Go in."

"Where?"

"The hole, of course." I just stood there and stared at it for a rally long time. Finally Ragnark decided to go ahead of me. He jumped and disappeared into the steam. Morn and Serrin followed. Steeling myself, I jumped into the hot rush of steam. It was only hot for a moment or two. Then it turned icy cold.

# Chapter 6
# The Nariss

I felt myself plunging downwards into the darkness. It was an almost vertical slope for a moment or two. Then it leveled out and curved sharply to the left. It was a tangled mess. I spiraled, curved and dropped into the dark. It was completely unlike anything I had ever experienced before, topping even the best of thrill rides. At times it was pitch black and all I could feel was rushing wind and turbulence. Sometimes, though there would be beams of blue or red light illuminating an old, cobwebbed tunnel, or allowing me some brief glimpse of something unidentifiable as I whizzed by. Once I thought I saw someone's skeleton. Mostly it was just a lot of darkness.

After what seemed like an eternity, I was finally rocketed out of the narrow tunnel. I flew through open air for a moment, then landed on the moist, cool ground. Serrin helped me to my feet. I guessed that I had to be a few hundred feet underground. Eerie blue light filtered in from some unknown source. As I dusted myself off, I noticed a series of holes in the wall behind me. When a Galian came flying out of one, I realized they were the tunnels that led to the surface. I seemed to be in a circular chamber of some sort.

We waited in the room for a little while until our forces were assembled. It was not the most comfortable place to wait. Chilling air flowed through the cobwebs. I kept feeling like someone was watching me, but when I looked up, it was nothing. I found it hard to believe that anyone or anything could live here.

At last the fairies began flying in swarms out of the holes. We were ready to go. As we set off down the spooky tunnel, Morn began explaining to me the role I was to play. I would pretend to be powerful sorcerer instead of a bumbling idiot. Morn would do most of the speaking , since I was still just getting acquainted with this world. All that was needed of me was to act mysterious and make whatever I did say sound dark and powerful. That, he explained, should scare them into joining forcers with us. He was whispering into my ear the whole time so as not to attract attention. "How did we wander this far in and not be attacked?" I pondered aloud.

"Oh, they're watching us." he whispered "If I hadn't been whispering this whole time, they probably would know the whole plan. I bet there's one following us right now." This prompted me to glance behind us.

We traveled farther and farther into the tunnel, which slanted ever so gently downwards. I brushed a cobweb away from my cheek and more than anything I wanted to be out of there. I suppressed a shudder as I ventured further into the darkness.

Something slimy brushed against my shoulder. I froze. I glanced fearfully over to my side. It was just a root, so I  brushed it away. It rolled back. Something was dripping on my head. I looked up and wished I hadn't.

It was possibly the ugliest thing I had ever seen. Its tentacle was dribbling down onto my shoulder. The remaining three held it to the ceiling. Its body was only remotely humanoid. It was disturbingly thin, especially around the waist. It snapped its jaws, sending foamy froth down the hallway. It slithered down  in front of me, its jet black body twisting in unhuman ways. It had a spiked tail that gave it balance. Two clawed feet held it upright. It reared back its head, which slided back into a crest. Its tongue, which seemed to have teeth of its own, flicked out for a moment. Clenching the claws on its hand into a fist, it hissed and began forming words.

"Who … goesss…thherrre?" it rasped. I almost fainted. Fortunately, Morn stepped in to help.

"We are a peaceful band of travelers," he said.

"You come … heavily armed," it replied. The glowing green slit on its forehead representing eyes seemed to scan the sword at my side.

"Necessary precautions," Morn briskly replied. The Nariss creature cut to the chase.

"Why … shouldn't I … kill … you all here?"

"That would be very unwise."

"Whyyy…?"

"You'd never make it alive." The creature chuckled. Three more Nariss surrounded us from all sides.

"Who … would neverrr ssurvive?"

"You underestimate us." said Morn. He was starting to sweat. "A powerful sorcerer is in our midst."

"You … lie."

Then the fairies swarmed in from all directions. "I believe," grinned Morn, "that you will recognize these fairies. The ones that you killed in Crescent Moon, the fairy village."

"Impossible!" yelled the creature, pointing at Mystique. "I killed her myself." his voice echoed through the halls. Mystique darted behind me at the sound of his voice.

"Obviously, it's not impossible."

43

"Who brought … them … back to life?"

"I did." I stepped forward, surprised that I was even bold enough to speak. The Nariss surveyed me.

"You are … puny." It was true. He – I think it was a he – was a good six or seven feet tall. Maybe even seven and a half.

"Maybe. But I could destroy you in an instant."

"Prove it." I had been afraid of something like this.

"Trust me, you don't want him to!" interjected Morn.

"Prove … it …" The creature looked at me with the slit on his forehead narrowing.

"Well," I said, suddenly getting a great idea. "How about I knock out one of the villagers using magic?" I beckoned to Ragnark, hoping he was catching on. He was. He begged in front of me.

"Please, master! Please! Not me!" he cried. Now, I was pretty much born into theatre, so I must admit that I was enjoying this part.

"Silence!" I yelled. Waving my hand around impressively, I thrust it towards Ragnark, who crumpled onto the ground in perfect timing. The creature was only mildly impressed.

"Mere … plllayacting … you could not … dessstroy one … of … us…"

"Fine then," I said, starting to panic. I realized that if I didn't do this just right, it might be the last thing I ever do. "I'll knock out one of you." I glanced around frantically. Then I relaxed as I saw Serrin, Bednik, and one of the villagers sneaking up behind one of the Nariss with clubs.

I waved my hand around impressively and then thrust it at the Nariss.  Fortunately, he crumpled to the ground silently. Now he was impressed. Morn breathed a sigh of relief.

"What … do you … want?"

"We want to see your leader."

Nodding his consent, the Nariss set off down the passageway. "Follow meee ..." it hissed.

We set off into the cool, misty darkness. There were fewer cobwebs as we got farther inside, but the atmosphere was hardly friendly. We went winding past multiple corridors. Finally we arrived at a pair of double doors.

The doors seemed to be carved of stone. With a single push from our guide's tentacle, they opened. Inside was a long hallway lined with alcoves. Inside the alcoves were statues of famous Narissian warriors. I could have sworn that some of them moved.

At the end of the hallway was another pair of stone doors carved in some strange writing. Another tap of the tentacle and these swung open as well.

We crowded out onto the cliff. The cliff ended abruptly and turned into an old, unstable suspension bridge. Then the bridge ended abruptly and became an ancient stone tower. Hundreds of feet above the top of the tower the ceiling curved into a dome. Hundreds of feet below the bridge, at the base of the tower, was a lot of boiling lava. Rushes of steam and fire shot up from the lava. Across the bridge at the top of the circular tower, was some sort of temple.

"I asssk ... that only ... five ... of yyyouu ... come across." it hissed. That meant me, Bednik, Serrin, Morn, and Ragnark could come across. The rest stayed behind.

The suspension bridge was extremely wobbly. It felt like it might give away at any moment. Somehow, we managed to make it to the other side.

We entered the old, musty temple. It was dark, but when our eyes adjusted we made out another Nariss sitting in a chair. He must have been about ten feet tall. Then I realized that his skin was a dark, rich purple instead of black like the others. He was obviously their leader.

Our guide knelt and spoke in some strange language that sounded like a computer CD-ROM being played on a CD player.

"What ... do ... you want, sssorcerer?" rasped the Nariss King. Morn nodded for me to speak.

"I want you to join forces with us."
"An ... allianccce?"

"Only a temporary one."

"Ifff you are ... sssuch a powerful sssorcerer ... then ... why do you ... need ... our help?"

"Our enemy is much stronger then us. They are stronger then you as well. And given time, they will obliterate you anyway. It is advantageous to both of us to join forces."

"That dependess ... nobody ... can defeat usss ... who isss ... thisss enemy?"

"Ranook and his undead."

"Ranook ... if Ranook ... should choossse to invade usss ... we will defeat ... him."

"If you were trapped in here, you wouldn't last very long." offered Bednik.

"Go ... before I ... dessstroy you." I was angry. Very angry. Without the Nariss, we didn't stand a chance against Ranook. For some reason, I focused on the temple wall. A brief wind ruffled my hair. I thought I blacked out for a moment. Then the wall exploded, shattering into a million pieces. Everyone froze.

"Join forces with us before I destroy you." I said through clenched teeth. He laughed.

"Go ... before I give ... the orders to kill ... your ... army." A tremendous force raged inside of me, as though I was trying to pry something loose. Then a pillar shook loose and fell directly towards the Narissian King!

# Chapter 7
# Uncomfortable Alliance

With all my might, I willed it to stop – and it did! It suspended itself in midair above the king's head. "Join us before you never have the chance to give that order." I panted. Somehow I was being weighted down as though the force of the pillar was upon me. Morn, Bednik, Ragnark, and Serrin stared at me with open expressions of shock on their faces. It could have been my imagination, but I could have sworn that I felt the sack Serrin had given me vibrating at my side.  Serrin would later swear that he had seen it glow red, too.

The king remained calm. "Interesssting … very well. Remove the … pillar … from above my head … and we sshall have … an agreement." completely exerting myself, I hauled the pillar back up into position … without even touching it. "Remove yourselvesss … and wait … for usss to join you."

We made our way back across the bridge to rejoin our group. I was very weak and stumbled across the whole way. A pair of Narissian guards led us to a shaft. An arch-shaped entryway led into the shaft, which appeared to be endless in either direction, vertically. Horizontally, though, it was very narrow. I started forward when one of the villagers was pushed in, but relaxed when she was instead sent screaming upwards. Serrin was prodded into the shaft and Ragnark, always the brave one, simply jumped in. Then I was pushed in before I knew what was happening. I floated on thin air for a moment, then shot upwards at an incredibly fast rate. There was single point of light above my head, and it was growing larger by the second. Then brilliant light surrounded me for a moment. I was being borne upwards in plumes of smoke. I was outside and it was dusk. Then the world came crashing down around me as I landed in a heap on the ground.

I heard applause explode around me. Ragnark and Serrin helped me to my feet. We sat down by the other villager. Then someone else shot out of the ground in a puff of smoke. We all clapped and cheered. Things went on like this until we had a whole audience of people clapping and cheering every time someone was ejected. The last person out was Morn. When he hit the ground, we gave a standing ovation. He took a gallant bow and brushed himself off. "We set up camp here!" he shouted. "Everyone at work!" Everyone shuffled to their various tasks. "Ragnark, Serrin, Bednik and Zephyr. You're with me." he added under his breath.

We pitched his tent and entered. A single green flame from a lantern illuminated the whole tent. The four of us sat down facing Morn. "All right," he said. "I want an explanation for what happened back there."

"Don't look at me," I shrugged. "I have no idea how I did all that stuff."

"Does anybody have any theories though?"

"Obviously he tapped into some kind of force," offered Bednik. "Though I've no idea what." there was a long pause.

"Well," sighed Morn. "If no one has any ideas, then I suggest that we all get to bed." We trooped out of his tent and into our own. Without a word between us, we rolled out our bedding supplies. I bundled up into mine as it began drizzling outside. It was a cold night.

The morning was still wet, cold, and rainy. We rose out of our beds and unpitched our tents. There seemed to be an unusual hurry about the camp, as though something was wrong. We struck camp quickly and ate breakfast while we waited for the Nariss. Our breakfast consisted of cereal, though it was certainly not the kind of cereal you're used to. The cereal itself was made of some crunchy species of nut which I had never eaten before, the clusters of which were suspended in dragon's milk. Dragon's milk tastes like an odd mix of chocolate, strawberries, and mint. There were also apple chunks that were fried in some sort of strange batter over the fire, orange juice to drink, and a few mugs of slurk that someone had stolen, thereby creating a black market in slurk for themselves.

Then a scout came running in, disrupting our meal. His clothes were torn and his raven black hair disheveled. There were tears in his eyes. "They're here!" he croaked. "T-they're here! Just a f-few m-minutes to the south!"

"Who's here?" someone said.

"The … the undead … the Cursed Ones …"

Then he fainted.

# Chapter 8
# Undead

The crowd went into a panic pretty fast. Morn came rushing over from a rock where he had been making battle plans with a couple of his officers.

"What's happening?" he growled.

"The Cursed Ones." I said, pointing to the guy on the ground. "He said that they're only a few minutes south."

"Where are the Nariss when you need them?" as if on cue, several Nariss flew out of the ground, further adding to the panic. As they came out, it became obvious that they were well prepared for battle. Somehow they had created weapons that could be integrated into the body. Arms were ending in scythes. Spikes adorned their backs. Their tales ended in maces. They were spewing out of the ground in almost undetectable blurs now, rapidly getting into formation as soon as they hit the ground. It was a well rehearsed routing. Finally, the king erupted from one of the mounds. He soared over the heads of his army, landing in front of them with a powerful thud.

"There you are!" shouted Morn, hurrying over to the king. "Listen, we have a group of undead headed our way right now! They'll be here any minute. We have to organize an attack now."

"Wherrre … are they … coming from?"

"South."

"Very well … we ssshall ssstay … here … and meet … them head on."

"Okay," he told his officers. "They're going to stay here and attack from the front. Serrin, I want you to organize your guard members and lay low on one side of the trail. I'll hold the other side. Where are the dragons?"

"Just out of sight, resting in the woods." replied an officer.

"Get them mobilized and in the air. I want them to attack from behind. Oh, and Zephyr, see if you can get the fairies to attack from above." I went to find the fairies while he continued giving instructions. It wasn't hard. They had found some blueberries on a plant and were munching away. "Mystique!"

"What?" she and a red-haired friend of hers had been in the process of tossing a blueberry back and forth. They were both smeared blue.

"Get in the air! Undead on the way—south. Attack them from…air." I panted, out of breath.

"I'm not going to do it," she said simply, tossing the blueberry back to her friend. The redheaded fairy, however, was unprepared, and was plucked out of the air by the berry.

"What do you mean?"

"I mean I don't see why I should risk my life and my people's lives to defend you."

"Second favor." I hissed.

"Oh, all right." she sighed. She began shouting out commands. Sometime when we weren't so rushed, I was going to have a word with her about gratitude.

Serrin grabbed me and shoved me into some bushes that lined a narrow trail, barely visible between the trees. Something was moving between the trees in the distance. The air grew steadily colder and I clutched the sword at my side. Peeking through the underbrush, I saw bones moving. Things moved in slow motion, as though in a nightmare.

Then an inhuman cry pierced the air. It meant that the undead had stumbled upon the Nariss. "Now!" I heard Serrin yell. Unsheathing my sword, I stood to my full height. It was one of the most – the most – terrifying thing I have ever seen.

Bits of rotting flesh hung from the skull. An eye was missing, so I was left staring at an empty socket. The skulls teeth were unusually sharp, and a pointed tongue could be seen rolling around in the mouth through some missing teeth. Decrepit rags took the place of actual clothing.

It craned its head at me ever so gently, and I heard creaking and snapping sounds coming from its pencil-thin neck. In a blue flash, I raised my sword. It held its cool stare for a fleeting second, not seeming to be afraid of anything. Then it seemed to implode as my sword struck it, the bones disintegrating in midair.

It was only then that I realized that I was surrounded by more than just one of the Cursed Ones. Starting to panic, I started frantically swinging the sword. Streaks of blue light dismembered one of the cursed ones every few seconds.

Then the fairies came. One of the undead was surrounded by glittering lights and hoisted into the sky, only to disintegrate with a terrible scream. Spearing another one in the chest, I watched the dust fall. Then a wall of flame erupted over my head, making my eyes water. The dragons had found the exposed rear of the undead.

The fighting was over as quickly as it had started. The only things left were piles of white powder that had previously been undead warriors and a few bones. I saw Bednik slice up a pile of bones that had been trying to pull itself together.

After dusting myself off, I saw Mystique hovering in front of my nose. "Nice job."

"Thanks," she grinned.

"Thank you for risking your …" it was starting to dawn on me. " … wait … you were flying too high for their weapons … and fairies can't have their souls sucked out! And you were making a big deal out of personal risk! You cheated me out of a favor!"

"Did I say anything like that?" she asked in her best sugary sweet I-don't-really-mean-it voice. "I don't think I did," and, smiling innocently, she fluttered off.

I met up with Morn, Serrin, Bednik, and Ragnark under a tree. The Nariss seemed engaged in some sort of odd victory ritual that involved beating each other over the head with their tails and the terrawumquazzalarneraphelliusdorimino'sa were circling high in the sky, apparently in their own victory celebration. A map was splayed on the ground, adorned by dotted lines and Xs. "Well done," said Serrin, barely even looking up at me as I approached.

"Thanks." I said, taking a seat around the map. "What's going on?"

"Just thinking about what Ragnark said earlier." replied Morn. "We've decided that we're going to go to Shanar and see if we can't recruit some more Glunches."

"And then?"

"And then," said Morn, grinning a sort of lopsided, crazy grin. "Then, we are going to go after the big cookie." I didn't need to be told who that was.

"Ranook." I said. He nodded. Ragnark, very interested in the part about Ranook, leaned forward.

"We can't just jump right to his castle." volunteered Ragnark. "We'll be spotted. We should take a more skewed path."

"Agreed." said Morn.

"Won't they spot us long before we arrive at the castle?" queried Bednik. Morn glanced up at the overcast sky.

"I don't think so." he said. He rolled up the map right as the hail began.

# Chapter 9
# Second Attack

I found myself staring at an impenetrable wall of gray. Wisps of fog curled around me. I felt the beating rush of wings on either side of me. I was numb with cold. The moisture splattered the goggles I had been given. The only warmth I felt was my own breath and the vague sensation of the terrawumquazzalarnerapheliusdorimino'sa beneath me. I was shivering, soaked to the bone. I could see the dragon's head more clearly as we emerged from the cloud. I ducked as a piece of hail the size of a basketball came flying over my head. I had one of the younger dragons, so I was the only one on him. The other dragons surrounded me. Serrin, Bednik, and one of the villagers pulled up alongside make on their yellow dragon. I could make out the fairies flying several feet above my head and the Nariss (they were very fast runners), down below.

"You holding out okay?" shouted Bednik.

"Not really." I yelled back.

"We'll land soon!" shouted Bednik. They pulled away. Then I noticed something moving on the ground. And it wasn't the Nariss. It was a familiar gray mass … fumbling with my telescope, I held it to my eye. A cold fear gripped me. Undead soldiers. Putting away my telescope, I yelled to Bednik. "I'm going down!" and cut into an almost vertical dive, dodging a stray flash of lightning along the way. I leveled over the head of the Narissian King. My dragon roared until he looked up. "Ready yourselves!" I yelled. "Cursed Ones dead ahead!" he nodded and I pulled up, realizing that I had just made a bit of a macabre pun.

I leveled alongside Serrin, Bednik, and the villager again. "What was that?" yelled Serrin.

"Undead." I yelled back, pointing to the gray mass. Serrin groaned. Then I heard something screeching.

"Terrawamnerapharquereneliusdorimno'sa!" groaned Serrin and Bednik together.

"What?" I said blankly.

"Dark Dragons." said Serrin.

"Assume defense positions!" I heard Morn yell. Then it happened. A missile composed of blue sparks and a trail of red smoke struck some Galian warriors on a dragon next to me. They and their dragons literally froze in midair and dropped towards the ground in a block of ice.

A moment later, I caught my first glimpse of a dark dragon. Well … not really. It was encased from fang to tail in armor. An undead warrior adorned its back. I heard weapons being unsheathed all around me and unsheathed my own sword. A volley of arrows plucked the rider off, sending it spiraling into the trees below. A blast of flame destroyed the dark dragon, instantly warming up my joints. A twisted hump of metal oozing some unearthly black material fell to the ground after its rider, crushing some of the Cursed Ones below. There was a long pause. "Is that it?" someone wondered aloud.

In response to their question, blue bolts struck us from all sides. We were plagued by dark dragons. Charging the nearest one, I knocked the rider off its saddle. I hacked at the armor on the dragon, but it was well made. It took me four strokes to get through.

On my fourth swing, I hacked through and was greeted by a thick, black fog like substance that dissipated as it hit the air. Screaming in agony, the creature was plucked out of the sky.

Having flames on our side was a great advantage, but it hardly helped. The air was saturated with dark dragons now. Something had to be done. We were dropping like flies. Each strike against the enemy had to be calculated for maximum effect. A single blast of fire from my dragon took out three dark dragons.

I don't much remember anything after that except blindly swinging my sword. I thrust it into the face of several terrawumnerapharquereneliusdorimino'sa, instantly plucking them out of the air. I was surrounded by them. No way out. The rush of beating wings filled the air. Tearing at my clothes … my face … my dragon …

I felt a surge rush in me, more powerful than any other before it. Pure, savage fury. There was a sudden flash of blue. White electric bolts attacked the undead. I had just enough time to see the bolts of lightning destroying dark dragons before I fell out of the saddle and blacked out.

# Chapter 10
# Darkness and Silence

A sharp yell cut the eerie, murky silence.

" … AT DO YOU … GAVE … THE …HIM?" was all I could make out.

" … don! It … I didn't think …be able …magic!" I was fading in and out, only able to make out bits and pieces of the conversation.

"Well … least now … that we're …going … camouflaged."

"Sorry …"

"And we … know why … keep … us so …"

"Ssh! He's … around!"

"So? Let … hear. He … right …know."

"No! If … knew … the story … would … us, and we … without him."

"Very … will not … him … now … soon …"

"Ssh!" I was beginning to recognize the voices. I stirred slightly. I opened my eyes. Two figures stood above me. One I recognized as Serrin. The other...I fell asleep.

When I next awoke, I was actually quite refreshed, but I stayed in bed for a little while, gathering my surroundings. I was in a tent, spread out on a cot. I was still quite damp and my clothes smelled like rainwater. A table lay by me. As I sat up, I saw my possessions laid out side by side. I stood all the way up.

After putting on my possessions, I ventured outside and was met by Morn, who was already helping himself to a cold breakfast of rakahn, a fruit in the shape of a spiral. I hadn't realized that I was hungry until I saw food.

I made a seat next to him, noticing the camp up and about. The fairies hid in the woods, but you could tell where they were because every so often a group of glittering lights would form into an amusing obscenity that is not fit to be written here. "Breakfast?" Morn offered. I took the rakahn and bit into it, washing it down with the proffered goblet of water. "Sorry," said Morn. "But we're moving under camouflage from now on because of the attacks. That means no more fires and no more fancy breakfasts." I nodded wordlessly, looking up into the clear sky.

"What happened?" I asked.

"What?"

"The battle."

"Oh." he took a deep breath. "Well, we weren't so lucky this time. We lost about thirty people."

"Out of how many?"

"About two hundred forty-five."

"That's not so bad, is it?"

"Against Ranook's forces it is. He's got hundreds of thousands of cursed ones."

"What's our next move?"

"We're going to the Undersky Straight, then through to Shanar, as soon as you're ready." I was ready. We packed quickly, and soon we were on our way, covering up our tracks as we went, with Serrin resolutely pulling the temple wall behind him.

Finally, we arrived at the Undersky Straight. It really should have occurred to me to ask what it was, but I pressed on anyway. Suddenly I was covered with shade. Looking up, I saw a bridge. It had a few supports rooted on the ground, but other than that, it stood pretty much on its own. Actually, I thought it was a roof until I heard people talk about the "Upside Down Bridge".

"Pardon me," I said to Bednik. "But what is this about the Upside Down…" my sentence was cut short as I felt the world swirl into a blur around me. An invisible force had kicked my feet out from under me. Everything swirled in my head. Then-WHAM! I came crashing back down like a ton of bricks. I quickly realized that I was sprawled out on wood, not dirt. Risking a glance upward, I saw…dirt. And trees. Lots of upside down trees. I stood up. And then I came to the realization that the trees weren't upside down—I was. It was as though gravity maintained its downward pull on my body, but it just couldn't pull me down. Swinging my arms above my head in a natural hanging position, I turned around and witnessed Bednik come flying from the ground to the bridge.

"That answer your question?" he said, calmly brushing himself off.

"Pretty much," I said, walking in a dangling fashion over the bridge. "Is it the bridge that's pulling me up?"

"No," he replied. "If the bridge wasn't here, you'd be falling into the sky." we traveled a bit further, then—"Look out for that missing board!" I jumped over a hole in the bridge and caught a fleeting glimpse of the sky.

Have you ever had your personal gravity reversed? If you have (perhaps you are reading this on the ceiling), try not to hop, skip, or jump. If my warning comes too late, try not to do it in an area where the sky is in open view underneath you. And *do not*, under *any* circumstances, have your gravity reversed outdoors. If you are floating on the ceiling right now, try letting go of this book. It is possible that the book merely had its own gravitational change.

Anyway, we walked a bit further and I felt my gravity shift again. Before I knew it, I had a mouthful of dirt.

As the sun set, Morn announced that we were nearing Shanar. "Put away any weapons you may have out," he said. "We want to appear friendly."

Within five minutes, we passed an old, worn, overgrown sign reading "Welcome to Shanar". Several huts lined a hill overhead. We were quite close to the sea now—I could smell it.

# Chapter 11
# Arrival in Shanar

"Yaaarrrggh!" the voice split the air like a knife. "Infiltrators! Sneak attackers! Traitors! Thieves! Burglars! Scumbags! Scoundrels! Robbers! Villains! I say, Gorlub, wake up! Offensive creatures!"

"Bulrog, what are you…"

"Quiet, Gorlub, I'm not done yet."

"But…"

"Red-handed sneaks! Vile filth! Despicable antagonists! Murderers! Crazed psychopaths! Diseased criminals!"

"Wait, Bulrog!"

"Never-do-wells! Evildoers! Super sneaky sneaking sneaks! HAVE AT THEE!" a pair of glowing red eyes—easily recognizable as those of a Glunch—came swinging out of the darkness at us, their owner following on a rope. The short little blur, still screaming a series of vehement insults, launched itself at us. The blade flashed towards us. I rapidly whipped out my sword and was copied by several Galian warriors standing nearby. "Sly demons! Morons! Imbecilic imbeciles!" WHAM! The speeding blur was disarmed in an instant. The blow that parried the blur's weapon also sent it flying in another direction—right into a great oak tree that blocked its path.

Another Glunch scurried down from the tree where he had been hiding. "Bulrog! I was trying to tell you—they're just another group of travelers!" Morn tried to give us a reproachful look, but he kept snickering. The taller Glunch helped the smaller one up. The shorter one wore a shirt with an embroidered B on the front. He hastily scrambled to retrieve his battleaxe. The taller of the two had a G embroidered on his shirt. The shorter one had short orange hair in a part down the middle. The taller one had purple hair in a ponytail, with bangs that hung down past his eyes. The shorter one had three small earrings in his left ear. The other one had a ring on his right eyebrow.

"Sorry about my brother Bulrog. He's—a little pessimistic." said the tall one.

"Sorry about my brother Gorlub. He's—a little too cheery." said the other.

"Wow—nice intro, Bulrog." I said. "I really admired your use of the word sneak."

"Thanks," he said.

"Please," said Gorlub. "Come rest. You must be tired." As we started up the hill, I started a conversation with Bulrog.

"You know," I said. "That intro needed something."

"What?"

"You should have called us bilabial fricatives somewhere."

"Whatsits?"

"Bilabial fricatives. It's the technical term for…" I blew a raspberry.

"Ah. I'll remember to call you that sometime!"

Our group was led up the hill to a bonfire. We met up with the villagers (who were quite enthusiastic) along the way. They were quite curious to see what was going on.

We had a dinner that was roasted over a bonfire that night. The whole village seemed quite eager to entertain and please. There were several songs and campfire skits. I even found myself telling a few stories and relying on my improvisational skills, which were met with hearty applause. There were a couple of little rascals who kept running up to me and poking me to see if I was real, and upon finding out that I was, made a hasty retreat, giggling furiously.

Soon our hosts insisted that the Galians sing a song. I vaguely remembered something about the Galians singing every morning, though I had never quite had the chance to observe the ritual myself.

As best I can recall, the song went something like this:

*On the full moon night of All Hallows Eve*
*Three brothers saw a prophecy*
*An ominous figure cloaked in red*
*Held the stone that bled*
*His cursed souls of fire*
*The ones that never tire*
*Would destroy and pillage*
*Every land and village*
*Bringing every land*
*Under the cloaked red hand*
*The three brothers sought to destroy him*
*Before he could destroy them*
*The Oracle knew they may not succeed*
*But to the Oracle they paid no heed*
*And now they are all dead*
*Thanks to the figure cloaked in red*
*Yet in their darkest hour*
*They cut a part of his power*

*In this goal they did succeed*
*So from enchantment they were freed*
*Instead released to the gates of death*
*Having done their last deed and*
*breathed their last breath*
*And the stolen fragment*
*Was stored in a tent*
*Until it made pilgrimage*
*To a nearby village*
*And there it stays today*
*Until someone comes its way*
*To avenge the dead*
*And destroy the figure cloaked in red*

It was beautifully sung in chorus. A few of the Galians had been appointed to play pan pipes or bells and the fairies were dancing above the fire. It sort of—well, more that sort of—violated our camouflage rule, but no one seemed to care. Morn himself led the chorus.

By now it was starting to drizzle, so we packed into the little bamboo cabins. Morn tried to tell Bulrog or Gorlub about out proposal, but was detained by a curious Ragnark. By the time we finally met up with them again, it was bedtime. Morn and I shared a cabin with Bulrog and Gorlub, and I distinctly heard Bulrog muttering "bilabial fricative" over and over again in his sleep.

# Chapter 12
# The Children

The next morning I awoke before anyone else, so I had a chance to get a good look at my surroundings. Bulrog and Gorlub lived in the same little hut, and you could tell. It was only a few rooms big, but the hut was divided in half. One half was disturbingly clean, and the other unscrupulously messy. One half had not so much as a piece of lint. The other had books and papers littered everywhere, cups half full of some murky substance, dirty clothes on the floor, grimy handprints on everything, overturned chairs and broken shelves. Of course the drawers were empty and had been gathering dust for ages. I figured that Bulrog's side of things would look more like my room if I had a house.

I ventured outside to view the partly cloudy sky. A few people were already out and about, namely the troublemakers who had been poking me the night before. They had now found an entirely different hobby. They had made a slingshot and found it amusing to sling small pebbles at me. I deprived them of their newfound hobby when they discovered that I, too, could throw stones, and with reasonable accuracy. I quickly chased away the three boys.

I soon found myself staring at the sea. A ship was harbored by the shore, gently swaying with the breeze.

I wandered the village for a little while, observing the quaint little shops and houses. Eventually I grew tired of strolling around and settled on the shade of a rakahn tree, wondering why none of the other early morning risers had opted to do so. It was a rather large tree, and the ripening fruits squirted a cool, colorful mist every few moments. I discovered why I was alone within the next ten minutes: a gaping hole in the trunk of the tree attempted to devour me. It was deprived of its meal, however, when I was rescued by a group of amused villagers, who quickly decided that it would be best if I instead chose the shade of a baby rakahn tree whose fruits still squirted the cool mist, but whose jaws had not yet grown.

Soon I found myself wandering the dirt roads of the village again. I was happening by the Jokes & Fireworks Factory when I heard a small boy scream. The source of the noise seemed to be coming from behind the shop, so I ran to investigate. Several villagers followed. When I got back there, I found myself face to face with one of the Nariss. A few of the villagers whipped out their weapons. And it looked quite suspicious, too: a little Glunch boy was being dangled by his foot. Two others held their slingshots out toward the small band of Nariss. "Put Jermy down!" yelled one of the little tots. Seeing themselves surrounded, the Nariss dropped the child (and none too gently, either).

"What's going on?" cried one of the villagers.

"We were…exxplorringg…and thessse chillldren…ssstartled usss."

The Nariss had been at the campfire the previous night, so most of the villagers sheathed their weapons. The three toddlers backed suspiciously into the group, still eyeing the Nariss. The Narissian who had spoken took a deep bow. "My apologiesss." he hissed, giving a bizarre smile. "They gave usss...quite a fright."

The group pretty much dispersed, but to those of us who stayed, it was quite obvious that the Narissians had given the kids a fright, not the other way around. Here I really met the four troublemakers who had poked me and thrown rocks at me. There was Jermy, an orange-haired tot. Tohma, who seemed to be the ringleader of the little group. Then there was Moguhn, who was a little shy, but a clever little jokester once you knew him.

Seeing that they were OK, I quickly parted ways with them, after making them promise not to throw any more stones. I wandered around until I wound up back at the hut.

When I got back inside, Morn and the others were already awake. I joined them for a quick breakfast consisting of hot cakes topped with dragon butter. Quite a meal.

After breakfast, we got down to business. "The reason we have come," offered Morn, "is to request your help."

"Then you shall have it!" responded Gorlub. Bulrog, however, was more reluctant:

"Anyone who asks help of me shall perish!" entirely ignoring the outburst, Morn kept talking.

"Long story short, we are looking for allies in a war against Ranook."

"RANOOK!" exclaimed Bulrog. "WE'LL ALL DIE! IT'LL BE A BLOODY MASSACRE! THERE'S NO WAY WE CAN WIN! WE'RE DOOMED!"

"Hmm..." said Gorlub. "Ranook...that might be tough, but I'm sure there's something we can do!"

"But Gorlub! What about the Trials?" a frown crossed Gorlub's face.

"I'm afraid Bulrog is right. There is the small matter of an ancient village law." I groaned. It was an ancient village law that had brought me here in the first place. "As the matter is," Gorlub continued, "the law says that one of you must endure the Trials of Alliance. It can get rather difficult, but I'm sure you'll make it!"

"It's no use!" interjected Bulrog. "You'll never make it! It's too difficult! You'll die! It's impossible to make it out alive! AAAAAAAAAAAHH—OW! GORLUB! What did you step on my foot for?"

We stepped outside while the brothers continued to argue. "Well," sighed Serrin. "Who's the lucky one?"

"I don't know." shrugged Morn. "Maybe we should draw straws."

"OK," I said. "Get me a pen and paper." Serrin chuckled, but Morn didn't get it. We eventually decided that we would hold a drawing at the campfire that night.

The rest of the day passed rather quickly. I spent it sword fighting with Ragnark, Bednik, and Serrin. We had a pretty good time, except that the rakahn tree kept trying to eat Serrin's sword.

The fire provided the only light in the entire village that night. The crowd twittered and shifted, obviously uneasy. They knew what was coming. Each of us, including me, had written our names down on a piece of paper and dropped it into a bowl. Part of me wanted to my name to be drawn, but the other part dreaded it. After everyone had dropped their names in and sat down, a very solemn-looking Morn reached his hand into the bowl. Too late it occurred to me that I should have written down Serrin's name and dropped it in instead.

Time seemed to slow down as the hand shuffled the names. After what seemed like an eternity, a piece of yellowed parchment was finally drawn from the bowl. Morn read it, shook his head a little, and whispered something to a couple of guards. They moved through the silent crowd. Something brought me out of my dreamlike state. It was a hand on my shoulder, pulling me up. The two guards started back toward Morn, with me in tow. *What was happening?* I shuddered and almost threw up as I realized that I was being chosen for the Trials of Alliance. Gorlub presented me with a medal. "You must wear this until the Trials," he said. Then he whispered, "Sorry." I just stared on in disbelief.

# Chapter 13
# Pirate Ship

I lay in bed that night, staring at the ceiling, fingering the medal, wondering what the next day would bring.

The next day, as it turned out, brought more than enough. I started the day out on a hilltop overlooking the village, watching the sun rise. The children played on the hill. Normally, I would have joined the festivities. Now, though, I was not in the mood. I noticed a small island on the horizon as the sun rose.

Breakfast was a hurried affair. I don't even remember what I ate.

Soon we boarded the ship. Gorlub gave us a quick rundown of what was to happen: I was to change into the outfit that challengers enduring the Trials were to wear; we would then sail to the island where the Trials were to take place. Several members from each of the parties interested in the Alliance would have to come, so I had to use another one of my fairy favors to get Mystique and her whole gang to come. However, nobody seemed willing to tell me what the Trials were going to be.

It turned out that the outfit made me look pretty much like a pirate. I wore a black jacket that hung open in the front. A long red cloth adorned my head, tied in such a manner that a tail of cloth a foot long hung down my back. A loose pair of gray pants covered my legs. The pants tucked into a fresh pair of boots. A pair of fingerless gloves protected my hands. I stepped onto the deck of the ship, looking and feeling very much like a pirate captain. I spotted Jermy, Tohma, and Moguhn playing on the deck and squatted down to talk to them.

"Hey, guys," I said. "How's it going?"

"OK." shrugged Tohma.

"Nice clothes!" grinned Moguhn.

"Yeah, I think so too." I said. "I look like a pirate, don't I?"

"Yeah!" echoed Jermy. "Like a pirate!" there was a long, uncomfortable pause. Then Jermy added, "What's a pirate?"

I quickly discovered that the crevice world didn't have pirates, so I set about explaining the concept immediately. The three tots latched on to the idea quickly. They soon decided that we should be pirates. They found a black cloth in the cargo hold and made me climb up top to tie it to the mast. I was dubbed "cap'n" and gave random orders which resulted in the kids swinging on ropes around the masts or yelling, "Aye, aye, cap'n!" and sliding to the deck below.

Serrin found us and was forced at imaginary sword point to join our swashbuckling crew of buccaneers (there was a lengthy imaginary swordfight before he agreed). We also captured Bednik and Morn and assimilated them to our crew, but Ragnark was nowhere to be found. Eventually we saw him emerge from somewhere in the cargo hold. He was promptly assaulted by a salty crew of pirates who forced him join our crew.

Right as Ragnark reached the crow's nest, a muffled boom sounded from somewhere below and the ship shook and vibrated. Ragnark fell from the mast, but turned his fall neatly into a dive, hitting the water in perfect form.

A giant ball of fire spewed from the ship, sending several sailors screaming into the water. This vibrated the mast so much that Moguhn fell into the water. Serrin dived in after him.

Risking a glance downwards, I saw a shower of sparks erupt from the ship. "Abandon ship!" could be heard over the din.

"Wow!" said Jermy, the danger of the situation completely lost on him.

"Neat!" added Tohma. "Just like a real pirate fight, huh?" colored sparks flew in all directions, igniting the gunpowder barrels used for the cannons aboard the ship.

"Jump!" I said. "Get off the ship!" sailors were jumping in all directions. Steeling myself, I prepared to jump. The sparks were replaced by jets of water spewing forty feet into the air. Another blast sent me and the remaining few toddlers reeling into the water.

The water rushed up to meet me. It was ice cold, shooting into me like a dagger. I plunged deeper. The water was blue, so I was not at all dry. The world now consisted of stinging sea salt and rushing bubbles. I lost sight of Jermy and Tohma.

I swam upward for an eternity, attempting to reach the inviting rays of sunlight piercing the surface. Finally I surfaced, coughing and sputtering. The mast of the ship stuck out at a forty-five degree angle. Plumes of smoke rose from the ship, sending a stunning display of fireworks into the air. The ship took on water fast. The mast sunk lower. The last few sailors jumped as a spectacular blast of flame heated the water all around us.

Then it was over. The water bubbled as the last traces of air escaped from the ship. The black flag slipped into the chilly water. "Well, that's just great! It's all over now!" boomed a voice beside me. I shifted to face it. It was Bulrog again.

"Now, now," comforted Gorlub from my other side. "It's really not quite so bad."

"Yes, Gorlub, it is!" moaned Bulrog. "It's at least a mile to shore for the Trials and three miles the other way! We'll be lucky if we don't drown or get eaten by sea creatures along the way! And, just to top it all off, there's a storm coming!" he was right. The sky was turning dark. We began swimming in the direction we had been sailing.

As we drew nearer to the island, I became eerily aware of the fact that there was a big rock on the island shaped like a skull. I also became aware of the fact that something was cutting through the water behind me. It appeared to be a red and black polka dotted dorsal fin. I tapped Gorlub on the shoulder. "What is *that?*" I asked. His eyes grew wide.

"That," Bulrog chimed in. "Is a pleasant, cheery little thing known as a…"

"SHRAK!" yelled a sailor. Right on cue, the shrak rose up out of the water. It was essentially a red and black shark with long, green tentacles. We swam faster. It was lunging left and right, attempting to eat some of our sailors.

Then another dorsal fin appeared. This one had a zebra pattern, only the background was green instead of white. I clutched a piece of driftwood just in time as the long rows of biting teeth and the tentacles rose up to meet me.

"HELP!" yelled a voice. To my surprise, it wasn't my voice. I glanced down. Moguhn was gripping the same piece of driftwood!

"You're alive!" I said, stating the obvious and momentarily forgetting about the big, scary monster chasing me. I only remembered when a shrak swallowed one of the sailors whole. A cold, slimy tentacle gripped my foot and tried to pull me of my piece of driftwood. It pulled hard. I, however, kept my grip, and so did Moguhn. As a result, the tentacle pulled me up, I pulled the driftwood up, and the driftwood pulled Moguhn up.

Luckily, however, the shrak noticed Morn thrashing his arms nearby and changed course, flinging us away. The piece of driftwood flew far, far away over the crowd, and skimmed onto the beach.

I would have collapsed right there, but I instantly remembered the rest of the toddlers and Serrin. My fear was relieved when a barrel rolled onto the beach. Serrin climbed out. He had a firm grip on Jermy and Tohma. *Then* I collapsed.

# Chapter 14
# Missing Items

I was first aware of lying on a hard surface; which was fine with me. I can't stand big, fluffy mattresses. I opened my eyes to the pattering of rain and the *crack* of thunder. A bright flash assaulted my eyes. I managed to peel my eyelids all the way open. I was lying in a chilly stone room. It was circular with a single window.

I stepped out the large oaken door. I was in a narrow hallway lined with torches. I heard arguing down the hallway. I slowly stepped down the hall, trying to shake off my grogginess. Eventually I stumbled upon an open door. Serrin, Bednik, Ragnark, Morn, Gorlub, and Bulrog sat around a table. One of Morn's servants was there, too. I recognized him as Naram.

"Oh, hello, Zephyr," said Gorlub cheerily. "Care for some tea?"

"*Tea!* He won't want tea! He'll want brandy!" I had tasted brandy once before and did not care to repeat the experience, so I was glad that Bulrog quickly found something else to object to.

"They have brandy here?" I asked.

"I'm afraid so," said Gorlub. "Legend has it that one of us went to your world and discovered the recipe. Vile stuff, though." I nodded. "There you are." he added, giving me my tea.

I casually sipped it, looking up at the ceiling, not really listening to the argument, which I think had something to do with who blew up the ship. All I remember was Bulrog insisted on contradicting everything that everyone said. I was busy thinking about the Trials of Alliance and what they would entail.

"Gorlub," I said. "What about the Trials? What are they going to involve?" he sighed.

"As much as I would like to tell you," he replied. "I'm afraid it's against the rules. What I can tell you is that this castle—Skull Castle, as it's called—was built specifically for the Trials. It's very complex. The designers included traps, puzzles, mazes, creatures, everything! Though, of course," he winked. "I can't tell you exactly what it involves."

I soon retired to my room to fall asleep to the pounding of the rain on my roof. I dreamed that I was asleep in my own bed.

I was being shaken. I awoke instantly. Bulrog's hand was on my shoulder.

"It's time," he said impressively.

"For what?" I said blankly.

"The Trials of Alliance, of course."

I was led down the hallway, my heart in my throat. Down a giant stone staircase that led to the massive entryway of the castle. A crowd was gathered there. A few had drowned when the ship sunk, but most everyone was there. From the back rows the Nariss watched. Glunches stood somewhere in the middle. Galians occupied the front row.

As the crowd parted to let me through, I could see Jermy, Tohma, and Moguhn right in front. Each bowed solemnly. Serrin, also on the front lines, gave me an oddly apologetic look and said, "Good luck, mate. Hope you make it out alive."

84

Bednik gave a deep, graceful bow. Ragnark saluted.

At last I was at the head of the crowd, facing Gorlub.

"You may take only one item to the first challenge. What will you take?" Two items leaped through my mind: my sword and the bag Serrin had given me. With my sword, I wouldn't have so much trouble with any creatures I encountered. On the other hand, Serrin had said that the bag would help me out if I got into a real pinch. Chances are I would be getting into a real pinch in the first challenge. I checked my belt for the bag. *It was gone.* I patted down my sides. It was nowhere to be found.

I couldn't have lost it at sea—I distinctly remembered having it on the beach before I fainted. I remembered it bouncing at my side before I went in for tea. What had happened to it? I checked around the floor. It wasn't there. I glanced all the way back up the staircase. It wasn't there.

"Whoa, hang on a second." I said. "I may have lost something. Can I go back upstairs to check for it?" Gorlub shook his head.

"I'm afraid not. You must go in now."

"All right, all right." I moaned. "I'll take my sword."

"Very well, then. The first challenge is the Maze of Death."

"Oh, joy. Sounds cheery." I was led to a big stone door which seemed to roll open on its own. Gorlub led me in.

"Good luck," he whispered. Then he stepped out.

# Chapter 15
# The Trials

The door slid shut with an uncomfortably final *thud*. No turning back now. I brushed a cobweb aside and moved forward.

The tunnel was dimly lit with flickering torches. It came to a fork up ahead. I paused for a moment, and then went left.

I proceeded down a mess of dimly lit passageways. Some went into dead ends. Others I did not venture down because a skeleton or bone or something that had once been a part of someone's body marked the entrance. At last I reached a hallway that looked promising. Then I saw three pits that extended down into inky blackness blocking my way.

I decided to double back and try the other passage in the fork. I went through endless passageways until I made it back to where I started.

This time I took the right fork. It twisted off into about twelve different passageways. Every single one of them was a dead end.

Finally I decided to go ahead and try to get over the pits. After what seemed like an hour, I made it back to the fork.

Again I took the left fork. I worked my way back until I found the pits. I leaned down and inspected them. The first was at least fifty feet deep, though I could not see the bottom. I glanced up. A root had somehow grown through a crack in the roof. I grabbed the root and pulled on it, putting all my weight on it. It held. Holding my breath, I swung across the pit, landing safely on the ledge that separated the first and second pits.

I let go of the root and searched for a way across the second pit. I checked the ceiling, which yielded no passage. Nothing on the floor either. Then I checked the walls. That proved to be my lucky break. The stone was cracked and uneven, providing plenty of footholds to climb across on. I almost slipped once or twice, but I managed.

Two down, one to go. I stood on the ledge between the second and third pits. There were no footholds on these walls, so I couldn't climb across. However, there was a beam in the ceiling; I thought that I might be able to pull it down and place it across the pit. When I pulled on it, it came down a short way, and then stopped, giving a loud *hiss*. An old wooden plank slid out the other side of the pit and stopped at my feet. *Well,* I thought. *That works.* I stepped onto the plank and walked across, balancing carefully. As soon as I set foot on the other side, it slid back.

The hallway made a sharp turn left. I found myself in a circular room. A set of stone steps led to a platform a few feet off the ground. There were four pedestals, each rising about three and a half or four feet off the platform. Each held a small bowl. Out of the first bowl shot a constant flame. Engraved on it was a symbol: it consisted of a box with three straight, angled lines sticking out the top of it.

The second one held water. The symbol on it was three zigzagged vertical lines.

The third basin held what appeared to be a noxious, poisonous fog with a blue color. The symbol on it was an X underneath two circles in a diamond.

The last basin held some odd, pitch black substance. It too had a symbol: two circles next to each other.

I was unable to make any sense out of these, so I continued out of the room and down the hallway. The hallway turned right and became a suspension bridge suspended over a maze. This portion of the maze had no roof, so I was able to chart a course before entering it. There was a doorway set into the wall on the right, so I assumed that was my goal and plotted the easiest possible course, bypassing any place with skeletons or other remains. Then I moved into the hallway at the end of the bridge.

I could see that the hallway went downwards into a stairway. Through a sort of window on the left, I could see that the stairway doubled back on itself and led into the maze.

Unfortunately, the walls were littered with holes and the halls were littered with skeletons. I picked up a handful of loose gravel and flung it down the hallway. Spears shot from the holes in the walls and retreated again before I could even blink.

"Well, fine then!" I said. "If you can shoot spears at me, I can cheat!"

I went back to the bridge and vaulted over the side, landing in the middle of my intended course. "Ha! So there!"

I continued down the course I had planned. Halfway through, I noticed a skeleton sliced neatly in half. I bent down and carefully inspected the floor and found a small slit. I carefully tiptoed over it, trying to avoid whatever trap was planted there. I felt as if I had been spotted by something. The hairs stood up on the back of my neck. Someone, or something, knew I was there. I took of running as fast as my legs would carry me. A series of circular blades sliced out of the floor, each one right on my heels. At last I saw (no pun intended) my destination. I reached the doorway and the circular saws sunk back into the floor, almost disappointed at having missed their intended target. I checked to make sure that I was all in one piece. Amazingly enough, all of my limbs and digits were still attached.

I stood there trembling for a moment, gathering my wits. Then I took stock of my surroundings. There was a symbol by the doorway. I quickly recognized it. It was two circles next to one another. It was from the fourth basin in the circular room. But what did it mean?

Still unable to make any sense out of it, I decided to continue on. The passage made a sharp right—and then went pitch black. The only light was the soft flickering glow coming from around the corner behind me.

Then I realized what the symbol must stand for: darkness! I turned around and went out of the dark portion of the maze. I tugged on one of the torches, but it wouldn't come off the wall. I tried three more torches. No luck. I was going to have to go through the maze in the dark. I re-entered the dark hallway.

Holding my breath, I stepped forward. I fully expected the path to drop out from under my feet at any moment. I made a sharp turn left and continued down the hallway, patting the walls with my hands. I could see nothing but black. I sincerely hoped that none of that spear-shooting-out-the-wall stuff would happen right now.

Then the real maze part began. The passages and hallways twisted and turned randomly. I sighed and wished for some light. Whenever I had done that sort of thing in this world, it had magically happened due to some sort of hidden power I possessed. I somehow slaughtered a whole army of dark dragons like that. I had almost killed the Narissian King. Maybe—just maybe—I could call on that power now to get some light. I concentrated really hard. *Light*, I thought. Nothing happened. "Light," I muttered. "Light!" I said, a little louder. Still nothing. "LIGHT!" I yelled. No luck.

I sighed and drew my sword, for no real reason. I was surprised to see that it was glowing. Not enough to really light the way, but just enough that if I held it to the wall, I could make out the cracks in the stone. That made me feel better instantly. At least until I saw the remains of the people who had taken this challenge and never made it out. There were no real traps in there, just the crusty old remains of people who had wandered about forever in there and never made it out. That made me feel right at home.

I wandered around for at least twenty minutes in there. Then I reached an area where a hole in the ceiling let in a shaft of light. Unfortunately, it shone down on a large pile of bones. They were wrapped in some slimy substance. And…were those *teeth marks* on them? A few of the corpses were plastered to the wall. I glanced up the hole in case it provided any avenue of escape. There was the roof of another room up there! I had found a way out!

*Clink.* Something moved in the darkness. I whisked my head out from under the beam of light and hid my sword. *Thunk!* There it was again!

I pressed myself into a small corner, trying to hide any trace of my presence. I heard a snarl in the dark. *Something was in here.* I saw a trace of movement on the other side of the light beam. Then a figure stepped into view. If you could call it that.

A pair of yellow, lizard-like eyes twisted and turned atop a long, narrow head. The jaw was adorned with sharp, twisted fangs and appeared to be oozing whatever was on the floor and walls. It was coated in yellow fur with blue spots. Two horns topped its head. It had a long neck and a big, hulking body. It walked on four legs and had two arms with razor sharp claws. To top it all off, it also had a tail like a mace.

It paused and grunted for a moment, trying to sniff me out. It knew I was there somewhere. I tightened my grip on my sword, ready to hack it to pieces if necessary. It drew closer…closer…WHAM! I made my attack.

Unfortunately, it anticipated my attack and blocked it with its tail. It used its fangs to counterattack, but I moved my head just in time. Then it swung its tail. I ducked down and the tail smashed into the wall behind me. I jabbed in the dark and was rewarded with a loud roar. The creature jumped back. It had a long gash in one of its legs that was bleeding black blood.

Now it was *really* mad. It roared with all its might and charged at me, swinging its tail, slashing its arms, and snapping its jaws. I thrust my sword forward and straight into its skull. It died with an agonizing shriek.

That being over with, I took another look up the hole. I could see no way up.

I soon decided to have a peek around the corner where the monster had come from. I was rewarded with a soft flicker of light from down the hall. I moved down the hall into what appeared to be the monster's lair.

A single torch on the wall illuminated the cold stone room. A pile of bones was slimed into one corner. On the opposite wall was a lever. I could see no skeletons around the lever, so I pulled it. It made a loud grinding sound, but other than that, nothing happened.

Dejected, I made my way back to the beam of light. A rope was sticking through the hole in the roof. I grabbed onto it and it began to pull upwards. I was dragged up through the hole.

Soon my eyes were assaulted by light. I jumped off the rope and landed on a stone floor. My eyes quickly adjusted. It was a circular room with a doorway, a torch, and nothing else.

I moved through the doorway and into a hallway. The floor was slanted upwards. Soon I arrived in a room with a fork in the path. Down one hallway was a skull engraved into the wall. Blue lighting was being projected onto it. Down the other hallway was an identical skull with red lighting projected onto it.

Two stone idols sat next to each other in the middle of the fork. "Well, hello." said the idol on the left. I blinked. *Did that idol just talk?* I stared at it.

"You'd think he never saw a stone idol talk before." said the one on the right.

"I-I haven't, actually." I said.

"One of us," said the idol on the left. "Must always tell the truth. The other must always lie. One path leads to safety, the other leads to destruction."

"That's correct." said Righty. "My path leads to safety."

"True," said Lefty. "But my path is safer."

"True," said Righty. "But mine is even safer than that."

"True," said Lefty. "But..."

"You're both lying!" I yelled.

"No we aren't!" said Righty. The ground trembled underneath me. A trapdoor opened in the ceiling. I was rising up on some sort of crude elevator.

"We aren't lying!" protested Lefty one last time. Then I was surrounded by darkness. I could feel myself moving up, but I could see nothing. Then another trapdoor opened above my head and I was pushed up through the floor of another room. I stepped off the stone block and it descended back into the shaft, the door closing after it.

Torches illuminated this room as well. A single doorway led out of the room. There was a symbol above the doorway. It was the three zigzagged lines from the basin with water in it.

I was afraid that I knew all too well what that meant, but I had to press on. Through the doorway was a hall that slanted down sharply. Soon it leveled out again.

Soon I began to feel something on my head. Some kind of dampness. I looked up and was greeted with a face full of water. It was pouring down now. I ran forwards. It wasn't long before I escaped the downpour. I flipped my bangs out of my eyes and looked back. Water was pouring down from the ceiling behind me.

Was I supposed to be scared of that? Then the second jet hit me. From the side this time. Then from under me. I ran through the maze, blinded by jets of water.

I quickly came to a realization: given time, the maze would flood. Now *this* was scary. I stumbled down the passageways, brushing water out of my eyes. Then I reached a dead end.

By now the water was about two inches high. I doubled back and pushed on slowly. I groped my way through the maze, trying to make out the water shapes.

I don't really remember much of that in great detail. I do remember, however, that the water was a constant threat. I felt it rise past my ankles. Past my shins. To my knees. Water was everywhere. Slipping desperately through the hallway, groping for a handhold. The water rose. Higher. Higher. Almost to my waist. A cold void of death at my stomach. A dead end. I doubled back. Another dead end. I doubled back again. Twisting passageways mimicked the knot that was in my stomach. Another dead end. The water was almost to my chest and slipping higher. I was wading now. Gasping for breath. A deluge of water poured down on my head. Another dead end. The water was coming up my nose. I held my breath and dived under. I kept swimming, hoping for a way out. Black corners lined my vision. I was almost out of air…blacking out…wishing I was home in bed, that when Serrin had asked me to follow him, I had flicked him away…then…*what was this?*…an upwards slope! I swam up…up…up…and I could breathe. I stumbled out of the water and collapsed on the cold stone floor.

*I could breathe!* It seemed like a miracle. I allowed myself a few moments to rest. Then I got up again. There was a lever by the wall. I pulled it, hoping nothing bad would happen. I heard the gurgling of water. When I turned around, I saw the water receding back down the passageway.

Brushing my wet hair out of my eyes, I continued down the hall. Soon I entered a circular room. There was a sudden, vibrating *THUD* from behind me. I whirled around. The path I had come from was blocked by a big, red, solid stone door. Next to it, apparently leading to another passage, was a blue stone door. About ten feet across from it was a stone idol. I pressed on the blue door. It wouldn't open.

"It's not that simple," said a deep, booming voice from behind me. *Not another talking idol*, I thought. I turned around. Yep—another talking idol. "You must first correctly answer a riddle."

"Uh...what will that do?" I asked.

"If you cannot answer it correctly, I will fry you on the spot with a fiery beam from my eye!"

"Oh, good, sounds lovely."

"Here is the riddle: I am a hard object. My first letter is R, my last two are CK. What am I?"

"A rock?"

"Correct. You may pass." I pushed the blue door. It didn't open.

"Uh...how do I pass?"

"*That* is not my concern." I just stood there for a few moments. Then I was struck by a sudden inspiration.

"Wait! Can I have the riddle again?"

"I am a hard object. My first letter is R, my last two are CK. What am I?"

"A dragon!"

"Incorrect!" I ran for it. A beam of red let erupted behind me as I hit the floor. The beam hit the door, which promptly exploded into a million pieces.

I stood up and brushed myself off. Then I casually strolled through the gaping hole. The door reconstructed itself behind me. I walked uphill for a little while until the passage leveled out. Then I approached another doorway with a symbol over it. This symbol was the box and the lines from the basin with the fire in it. Through the doorway was a long, winding hallway with cobblestones on the floor. All the cobblestones were red, save for a few that were blue. I picked up some loose gravel. One piece I tossed on a blue stone. Nothing happened. Another I threw on a red stone. Fire erupted from nowhere, momentarily obscuring the hallway from view.

As soon as it cleared, I jumped onto a blue stone. Then the next one. Then the next. So far, so good. I jumped onto another one.

The end of the hallway was in sight and I was merrily hopping along when *oops*, my foot decided to step on a red stone. A blazing heat erupted behind me. I ran. The hallway turned a fiery reddish orange. I dashed out the exit and hit the floor, my hands covering my head.

A heat wave burst over me, thoroughly drying me off. Soon it was over. I stood up and dusted myself off for the umpteenth time, then continued down the passage.

I rounded a few corners through a simple maze, nothing too complex. It occurred to me that I was really thirsty by now. Finally, I faced a long, narrow passage. Another symbol adorned the entryway to this passage: two circles in a diamond above an X. This had to be from the fourth basin. The one with the blue fog in it. This made me feel uncomfortable, but I had to proceed.

I stepped into the hallway and a stone door slid shut behind me. Noxious looking blue fog slipped into the hall through invisible cracks. I took a deep breath, held it, and ran for the end of the hallway. It seemed to take forever to get there. I kept running. The end of the hall refused to budge. In fact, unless I was mistaken, it was actually *shrinking*. There was no doubt about it—the further I ran, the further it got. I tried walking backwards. The end grew the teensiest bit closer. I ran backwards. Soon I arrived at the end of the hallway and rounded a corner. A door slid shut behind me, sealing off the poison.

Now I was in a simple room with a natural basin on either side of it. Each basin extended the full length of the room, was about three feet high, and held water. I rushed gratefully to the water for a drink. As soon as I picked some up in my cupped hands, I was struck by an eerie feeling. I dropped the water. Each end of the room was closed off by a door, so I ventured to the end I had not come from. It opened and I stepped inside a dark passage. As soon as it closed, I saw a skeleton on the floor. The poor guy looked like he'd had his flesh eaten away. He was holding a sign carefully scribbled on parchment during his last moments: *Don't drink the water.*

I stepped into a circular room with nothing in it. The floor made grinding noises and started to descend.

Suddenly, I was back in the main room of the castle, descending from the ceiling. The crowd erupted into cheers.

# Chapter 16
# A Wrong Turn

The crowd cleared a little spot for the platform to land. Jermy, Tohma, and Moguhn were waving homemade pirate flags. Bednik, Ragnark, and Serrin were ecstatic. Gorlub looked really happy, but I think Bulrog was expecting more death.

"You did it, mate!" yelled Serrin.

"Well done," said Bednik.

"Excellent job," added Ragnark.

"I knew you could do it!" blurted Serrin. "That's why most of us put your name in instead of…" he was interrupted by a stomp on the foot from Ragnark.

"You *what?*" I yelled.

"I mean, uh…nice weather we're having, isn't it?" Now I was sure that I should have written down Serrin's name and stuck it in the bowl.

After I had taken a good long nap, there was a feast. We had some kind of pancake thingy that tasted like bananas and oranges, flasks and goblets filled with slurk and dragon's milk. There were pies topped with cream, various kinds of bread soaked in butter, hot soups with cheese and spices, and icy cold deserts. I also seem to recall a Glunch-shaped cake that was dancing and singing a little ditty. Bednik got the head and we could hear songs coming from his stomach all night. There was some Narissian food too, but most of us avoided it, as it appeared to have put up quite a fight before becoming food. I started losing my appetite when the gelatin began performing acrobatic tricks. It brought new meaning to the phrase "Dinner Show."

"Pardon me, everyone," announced Gorlub. "I have an announcement to make: the remaining two challenges of the Trials have been cancelled!"

"WHAT?" yelled Bulrog. The resounding cheers soon drowned out his protests. I also cheered, but I decided that I'd best retire when my soup burped.

I moved back up the stairs to my room, wondering where all that food had come from, then deciding not to think about it, since most of it had been moving or talking.

Finally I found my little chamber away from all the excitement. A glance at the window revealed that it was night now. Of course it was still raining—that seemed to be the weather's general disposition around here. I lay down and yawned, wondering when I would get back home.

The first thing I was aware of after that was something hard on my chest. I gradually fluttered awake and rolled over. The sharp, jabbing intrusion was gone now. I looked beside me. Serrin's bag! It was back! I must have rolled over onto it. I tucked it into my belt and ran outside the room, barging down the hallway. Everyone was gathered at the base of the stairs again. I met Serrin after I slid down the banner and almost crashed into him.

"Hey, Serrin!"

"Hmm?"

"Guess what?"

"What?"

"I found the bag you gave me!"

"Oh, good! Where was it?"

"I don't know, actually. I just rolled over this morning and it was under me."

"Odd. Listen, I was just about to come wake you. A ship from the village came last night. They're going to take us back. Have you got everything?"

"I think so."

"Good. Off we go!" we stepped out into the rain. I was half expecting the ship to blow up, sink, or get attacked by shraks before we even got there, but the trip passed uneventfully.

Soon we arrived back at Shanar. As soon as we were off the ship, Morn was shouting out orders left and right.

"What's going on?" I asked Ragnark.

"We're setting off for the castle." he responded. I had hoped to catch some rest, but we were rushed onto the warpath, covering up our tracks as we went.

We walked for quite a while. Nothing really happened until dusk, so I will skip to that. I am sure you do not want to read a book about me walking. If you did, you would have picked up an exercise book and glued my picture in it. And then I would want to know where you got my picture. Maybe you got it from this book somewhere. If that is the case, then you would not want to read a book about me walking in the first place.

Anyway, that afternoon we were walking along. The afternoon was beginning to blend into evening. I was thinking—daydreaming—about something, but I don't remember what. Maybe it was about an exercise book with my picture in it. Anyway, I got distracted, like many people who daydream. The people marching with me got fewer and fewer, but I didn't really notice. I was given a sudden nasty jolt when I realized that I was wandering through the forest at dusk with not a soul in sight. Naturally, I was slightly— okay, *very*—uncomfortable.

I began to panic and started running, shouting out the names of everyone I knew, hoping somebody was around. WHAM! I bumped into something hard. I whipped my head around and found myself staring at a door. Two yellow squares of light representing windows, one on either side of the door, cut through the darkness. I was staring at a small hut. I knocked on the door.

A small man answered the door. He was another Glunch clothed in dirty rags with a round, smiling face and a pudgy body. His hair was orange and curly.

"Why, hello." he said. "You must be lost. Come on in!"

"How did you know I'm lost?"

"You must be! Only people who have hopelessly lost the way can find my house." I stepped inside. It was a little hut with a few candles lighting it. The walls were painted yellow with a big purple spiral moving throughout the room. The furniture looked very large and comfortable, though it was all slightly askew and unsymmetrical. And there were lots of clocks. Clocks on the walls, watches on the tables, even a sundial or two. Each timepiece had a different time.

"What's your name?" I asked.

"Tronks," he said proudly. "What is yours?"

"Zephyr."

"Oh, look, Zephyr, it's time for tea!" he said, randomly pointing at a clock. He led me into the kitchen. The kitchen was painted orange with green polka dots. There were no clocks in this room, but there was a star-shaped table with some octagonal chairs.

I sat down in one of the chairs (which was surprisingly comfortable for an octagon) and Tronks served tea out of a gold, silver, and purple tea set. "So, you're human, then?" he asked.

"Yes."

"Interesting. The last time a human dropped in was several months back. Young fellow. Teenager. About your height. He came from a place on Earth you call...Japan, I think? Went by the name of...let's see...by the name of Keisuke, if I remember correctly. I think he signed my guest book." the odd little man clapped his hands. An old leather-bound volume materialized out of nowhere and fell onto his lap. It had to be at least a thousand pages thick. "Here," he said. "You sign too." he flipped it open to a page with a blank line. I quickly scrawled my signature. He snapped it shut and I was left wondering how on Earth a quill had gotten into my hand. It seemed to have materialized out of nowhere. When I looked up, the guest book was gone.

I sipped the tea. It tasted like cinnamon. Tronks checked a pocket watch that was tucked away in a pocket of his velvet coat. *Wasn't he just wearing rags?* I thought. "Oh, look! It's naptime!" he said.

"I thought it was teatime." he checked a different timepiece.

"No, we're both wrong! It's time for breakfast."

"Are you sure?"

"Let me check." he glanced at his wristwatch. "No, it's hattime."

"What's hattime?" I inquired. He clapped twice. Several hat racks appeared around us. Each rack bore a variety of hats and caps of all shapes, sizes, colors, and designs.

"Hattime," he said. "Is when you must wear as many of these hats as possible." he grabbed a red felt cap and slapped it on, then put a black top hat on top of it.

I threw on a purple top hat and added a blue felt cap and a black and white bowler on top of that.

Before long, Tronks was wearing a stack of hats twice as high as himself. I added a red and green checkered beanie on top of my hats and twirled the propeller. It actually lifted me off the ground a couple of feet. Soon we were both teetering and tottering left and right. The hats toppled around dangerously on top of our heads. I attempted to drink tea while wearing thirty hats. Do *not* try this at home.

Our little party was interrupted by a sudden *crash*. Tronks and I teetered into the room where the crash had come from. This room was painted in green and red candy cane stripes. A large cloud of golden dust was rising from the fireplace. A human form stepped out of the fireplace, coughing and sputtering. She was Japanese, about eleven or twelve. She brushed the soot out of her short black hair, then looked around the room. She was the first human being I'd seen in a long time. She caught sight of us and started giggling. Then she fell flat on the floor laughing at the sight of us wearing all those hats. "Another visitor!" cried Tronks, not in the least bit startled. "Welcome, welcome! Oh, dear, you don't have a hat! Here, take one of mine." he gave her an oversized fuzzy pink top hat which promptly slipped over her still-laughing face.

"She's gotten lost somewhere in your world," he explained. Suddenly it occurred to me that too much time had passed since I had arrived in Tronks' house. I had to find my way back to the main group, if I could.

"Listen, Tronks, sorry to disappoint you, but I have to leave soon, or else I may never get back." I promptly toppled under the weight of all those hats. The small Japanese girl began trying on the ones that I had dropped. She caught sight of herself in a mirror and burst out laughing again. I was certain there had been no mirror when I had entered the room.

"Leaving so soon? Very well, very well. Come on, then," he led me back to the main door and I stepped out. "And remember," he added. "If you ever find that you need to get truly lost, just come find me." I supposed that was his way of saying goodbye.

"So long, Tronks…" I fell down a massive hill which had *definitely* not been there before. I sat dazed at the base of the hill. Tronks merrily waved goodbye from his doorway.

"Zephyr!" hissed a voice behind me. I whirled around to face the speaker and relaxed when I saw who it was.

"Ragnark! Don't do that to people."

"Sorry. I was wondering where you were. Didn't see you for the last several miles. Where were you?"

"Actually, I was…" I jerked my thumb over my shoulder and turned my head to face that direction. The curious little hut was no longer there.

"You were…" prompted Ragnark.

"Never mind. I must have taken a wrong turn."

# Chapter 17
# Rain

By the time Ragnark showed me where camp was, most of the work setting up had already been done (which was fine with me, as I am not a big fan of actual work). I found Serrin and Bednik arguing with the fairies about why the fairies couldn't play ball with our supply of berries. This left Mystique and her friends sulking.

When dinner was done, we sat down on logs and ate a hushed meal. It was a cold dinner, but the cooks had done wonders with some salty crackers and soup with bread flavored with nuts and berries.

Before long it was drizzling again. Then the lightning started. The whole crew was used to this sort of weather, so nobody really paid much attention. However, the lightning illuminated something in the distance. It appeared to be a tower. We were far away, but I could easily tell it was the biggest thing I had ever laid eyes on—maybe hundreds of stories high. I nudged Serrin, who was sitting next to me, stuffing his face with bread.

"Serrin," I said. "What's that?" right on cue, a flash of lightning illuminated the tower. He swallowed a mouthful of bread.

"That," he said. "Is the castle of Ranook, if I know my stories right. They say that the tower is several hundred stories high. He sits in the top story, watching and waiting."

"Waiting? For what?" Flustered, Serrin began munching again and didn't answer. Ragnark and Bednik sat on a log, staring at the tower, holding a hushed conversation that I couldn't hear.

Five watchmen stayed up that night in shifts. We slept on the fresh, simple, mossy earth, the cold rain pelting our faces.

The next morning was also cold, and the presence of the dark tower kept a constantly dark eye on us, though none of us dared to look at it. We packed camp before we even ate breakfast, ready to go at the slightest noise. We ate something cold—I don't even remember what it was—while we marched towards the castle. It felt like we were marching into the cold hands of death. None of us took our eyes off the ground, except Ragnark, who seemed to be holding a staring contest with the castle. He stared at it defiantly, as though challenging some unknown person inside.

It seemed that I had scarcely started walking than I found myself at a pair of wrought iron gates, overgrown with vines, tangled roots, and ivy. Just beyond it was the castle, looming over what had once been a town, but was not completely deserted.

Morn, who was at the head of the group in front of me, stopped and stared, not quite sure what to do. Then, after wrestling with himself for a moment, he gave it a push. The gate yawned open, inviting us to enter its cold jaws.

We entered the old, abandoned village without a trace of resistance. Old carts with faded signs offering fruits and goods had long since been devoured by time. They stood in unorganized rows in front of old buildings and huts where families had once lived, but had been unoccupied for so long they were now uninhabitable.

By now our whole army had entered, yet everything was still silent as a ghost. The fairies flitted overhead, not making any audible sound. Without any audible command, we stopped. There was no life, no sound, and no movement. Something was very wrong.

Without warning, the gate slammed shut behind us. Thousands of Cursed Ones rolled out from under carts, rose up from behind them, leaped out windows and doors, swarmed out of the castle. We were surrounded and outnumbered. I was too horrified to move. Then, somehow, I found the will to draw my sword.

Within moments, I found myself hacking away at the undead. Since we were drastically outnumbered, they managed to split us up into groups, which grew smaller and smaller during the confusion. Within a minute, I was on my own, surrounded by a horde of eerie skeletal warriors, leering at me through empty sockets. The remains of what had once been my comrades were flying through the air, departing from life before even hitting the ground. Each time I saw it happen, I would swing harder.

I managed to fight my way back to Ragnark. We fought our way back to Bednik, Morn, and Serrin.

No words were spoken. I decided that I'd had enough. I set my eyes on the entrance to the castle, which was guarded by a cloaked stone figure on either side. I decided that I would make it there.

Suddenly, I was doing it. I was fighting through crowds of undead, my four comrades at my heels. *I was there. I had entered the castle.*

The hallway was lined with skull-shaped torches. Each torched burned with some unnatural blackish-purple flame, illuminating the large hall with an eerie glow. The whole place was full of cobwebs. Skeletons hung from the walls and ceiling.

"Cheery fellow, isn't he?" said Ragnark.

No sooner had he spoken than we were attacked on all sides by raging undead that had appeared from nowhere. A few even dropped down from the arched ceiling. Morn took something out of his knapsack. It looked like a smoking cylinder. With a mighty roar, he hurled it into the midst of the undead standing in the entryway to the castle. A second later, they were torn from limb to limb by a giant ball of fire. Unfortunately, the entrance to the castle was very old. The force from the bomb sent it caving in, cutting us off from the outside.

"Well, that was just what we needed!" said Bednik sarcastically.

"At least none of the Cursed Ones can get in from the outside." offered Morn apologetically.

"In the meantime," said Serrin. "We're stuck in here with hundreds more, and only one of us has a truly effective weapon!" I hacked apart another skeleton as it came at me with a scythe.

There was really nothing anyone else could do, except lure the undead away from me while I attacked more of them.

Finally we cleared the hall of Cursed Ones. We proceeded cautiously down the gothic hallway, climbing a set of stairs. Serrin found a window. We peered out. We were probably about five stories up by now, with a good view of the battlefield. The dragons were swooping down out of the sky, frying dozens of undead in one swift move. Every so often, the fairies would drop down and pluck a Cursed One off the ground, disintegrating it in midair. We moved on quickly.

The castle was a literal maze. We found our way through the dungeons easily, though a few undead popped out at us from behind corners. Soon we found ourselves climbing an endless spiral staircase lit by the eerie black torches.  A few Cursed Ones blocked our way, but nothing much. The going was getting easier.

Then the staircase came to an end. We were in another stone room with a high, arched roof. The room was wide and circular. There was no door out. In the middle of the room was a cylindrical basin four feet high. It was filled with a metallic blue liquid that rippled and moved in curious ways.

That was the only observation I had time to make before the wall behind us was destroyed by a giant fireball. The blast threw us onto the ground. As the smoke cleared and the debris fell, I could make out something massive. It was a dragon's head. Two figures materialized from the smoke cloud…it was Gorlub and Bulrog.

"There *had* to be a better way to do that." grumbled Bulrog.

"Hello, there!" said Gorlub in a remarkably cheery voice for someone who had spent the day fighting a massive army of skeletons. Behind them was a gray, cloudy sky. The dragon flew away. "Thought you might be needing a hand," he continued. "We saw you disappear in the doorway and decided to come after you. Got lucky with that way, though."

"I'll say." replied Bednik. "You're lucky not to have crushed us!"

"What was that noise?" said Ragnark.

"What noise?" said Serrin.

Without further warning, a massive group of Cursed Ones flooded the room from the staircase. They didn't charge directly at us, though. They circled around us while more came in. We were literally surrounded by a group of undead five ranks deep.

"Well, that's just *great*." grumbled Bulrog as they marched in.

"Don't worry, we can make it!" countered his brother.

"No, we can't!" he shouted. "We're surrounded! Zephyr's weapon is the only one that works against them, and even if we were to discover that this metallic blue liquid would somehow transform our weapons so that they would work against the undead, which it wont, we're still outnumbered drastically!" he stopped to take a breath. By now the undead were so close that I was almost face-to-face with them. "In short," he continued. "WE'RE DOOMED! DOOMED, I TELL YOU, DOOMED!" On the last *doomed*, he collapsed dramatically onto his knees and threw his axe high into the air. It landed in the liquid, stopping a foot deep. The blade instantly turned blue like that of my sword.

I grabbed the hilt and swung the axe at the nearest Cursed One. It sliced and disintegrated the skeleton. Just like my sword. Bulrog grabbed his axe and I swung my sword like crazy. However, the axe proved to be too heavy for him. Even as I was engaged in fighting, I could remember the side effect of the spell that made my sword so effective. Seeing that he wouldn't be able to wield it, I snatched the axe from him and fought the undead with two weapons.

Once again, I was the only one fighting. Then I was joined by someone else. I couldn't believe it! There was another streak of blue metal destroying the undead in an instant! My eyes bulged when I realized that it was an arm. Ragnark's arm. There he was, standing right next to me, with a blue, metallic right arm!

"What did you do?" I yelled in the din. "Dip your arm in that stuff?"

"Pretty much." he said nonchalantly. "All I do is touch them and they die. Listen—I think we can clear a path to the busted wall."

"And then what?"

"Call a dragon to get us out of here, maybe?" it was the best idea we had. More undead were pouring in every minute. Five more minutes and we would be goners. We protected the others and forged our way through the crowd as best we could. It was an impossible task. Each skeleton we hacked away was replaced by another one.

As it turned out, the others weren't totally useless. Morn saw the difficulty we were having and took out two of his pocket bombs. He hurled the smoking cylinders into the stairwell. An undead caught one of the cylinders and peered at it quizzically. Then it blew up in the Cursed One's face. The other one also set off a massive explosion. For a moment, it was too bright to see. The room was filled with smoke, sparks, and fire. Then the flames cleared. Half the undead were gone. The staircase was crumbling. Several cracks lined the floor. One of the columns supporting the room crumbled and fell into the staircase, blocking it against the Cursed Ones. Ragnark and I fought like crazy to get to the opening in the wall. We made it there in a matter of seconds. Serrin whistled loudly.

A few seconds later, two dragons appeared, their beating wings causing a rush of wind on our faces. Ragnark jumped out the opening and grabbed onto the leg of one of the dragons. The other dragon joined legs with the first one by whipping its claws around the first dragon's leg. Serrin leaped out the window and grabbed onto Ragnark's legs. The dragons started to move upward. Bednik jumped out and grabbed onto Serrin's legs. I leaped out over the abyss and grabbed onto his legs. Morn grabbed my legs and Gorlub and Bulrog came last.

The dragons steadily beat their wings. We rocketed ten stories higher.  Then another ten. And another. I was being pulled even higher, the wind beating down on my face. Then we stopped. We were only a few feet from the roof of the massive structure. The battlefield was a mere speck below, with soldiers the size of ants swarming around. The moisture from the clouds dripped onto our faces.

"Let's drop off here!" yelled Ragnark, nodding to a window adorned by a gargoyle. Bulrog swung his body back and forth, gaining momentum. Then he let go of the chain and went sailing into the window. Gorlub followed. Morn swung in with ease. I rocked back and forth…back and forth…I let go. I went sailing in the window and landed on the cold stone floor, then rolled out of the way. Within moments the others had joined us. The room was about thirty feet high with a flat ceiling. The window I had jumped in was near the top. The room was circular. A table adorned the middle. It looked like the table had once been eaten upon, bit had not been used for a very long time. The ceiling was engraved with a picture of the tower. A huge demon of some kind stood at the top of the tower, looking out over the land. Several suits of armor stood on one side of the room. A closet was on the other. A small cot was tucked away against the wall.

"It's a room," I breathed. "Someone lives in here."

"Very astute," came the cold reply. We whirled around. A red cloak was gliding out of the shadows. Each step it took we stepped back. Then it stopped. Two gloved hands removed the hood. Underneath was a mask made of solid metal. It was a mask shaped like a skull, only the canines were long fangs and the eyes were two evil slits. "It is *my* room." continued the cold, penetrating voice behind the mask.

"Ranook." breathed Serrin.

# Chapter 18
# Ranook

"Correct." replied the cloaked figure. "I believe thanks are in order. You have brought me my power. *And* my brother." he shot a cold, calculating glance at Ragnark.

"Separated at birth." said Ragnark.

"And now reunited." said Ranook. "You have a choice. Serve me or die."

"Serve you?" Ragnark gave an evil laugh. "I already have been from the start!"

And then it came to me. "It was *you* who blew up the ship!" I yelled. "I saw you come out of the cargo hold right before it blew up! And it was you who took my bag before the trials! You kept giving our location to Ranook!"

He gave a dry chuckle. "Too bad it took you too long to figure it out!"

"I'm impressed." said Ranook. "However, I believe this human boy has something I need. Bring it here." Ragnark grabbed me and ripped the bag from my side. Ranook took out a similar bag and opened it. He pulled out a stone. The stone was blood red and constantly swirled in patterns under the surface. A large chink was missing in the side. He gave it to Ragnark. "I will reward you by letting you do the honors."

Ragnark opened my bag and took out a stone—one the exact shape and size of the chink in the larger stone—and slipped it into the stone. It fused together effortlessly. Ranook turned his attention towards us.

"You hid this from us?" yelled Morn.

"Not *all* of us." said Bednik uncomfortably.

"You knew?" I shouted.

"Yes." he sighed. "But...I didn't think...I...I...never knew he would do *this*." the stone was changing color, becoming lighter.

"And *you!*" I yelled at Serrin. "You gave me the Bloodlust Stone? Why? Did you actually want Ranook to find me and kill me?"

"I...um..." he wasn't paying attention to me. He was looking at something else. I followed his gaze. Ranook was advancing on us, his sword drawn. It was a wicked looking thing. The serrated blade was curved back and forth like a snake. Several chinks had been deliberately carved into the blade.

He raised the weapon, about to strike the final blow. Then a blue streak flew over his head, landing neatly in Morn's hand. It was the Bloodlust Stone. Somehow, it had changed color and was pulsing blue. Ranook whirled around in horror. Ragnark stood there, casually grinning.

"Traitor!" roared Ranook.

"Quit whining," said Ragnark. "It didn't belong to you anyway."

Ranook charged, emitting a horrible roar. A peal of thunder sounded outside. This time it was my turn to think fast. I threw Bulrog's axe over Ranook's head. Ragnark caught it with ease. He parried the blow from Ranook with his blue arm. My sword whirled into action, almost on its own, as though it was made specifically for this task. Ranook whirled to face me right on cue and parried my blow with incredible force, sending a vibration through every muscle in my body.

Wisely enough, Ranook got out from between Ragnark and me. He made a break for it, and, with a massive leap, jumped out the window.

"So...does that mean you didn't blow up the ship or take my bag?"

"No, but I have a good idea who did."

"Who?"

"I'll tell you after we take him down." he said, casting a discreet glance at Serrin.

There were plenty of footholds on the wall, so we were standing on the windowsill in a matter of seconds. I took a quick moment to review the battlefield below. We were winning. Now that the stone was on our side, the undead were scattered and confused.

"There he is!" yelled Ragnark. I glanced up, the heavy rain assaulting my eyes. There was Ranook, scaling the last few feet to the roof.

Ragnark grabbed the wing of an oversized gargoyle and hoisted himself onto it. He helped me up. We only had about ten feet to go to the roof. There were enough footholds to climb, but the rain made it difficult. I almost slipped several times. Somehow, Ragnark and I managed to pull ourselves onto the roof.

Ranook was waiting. Wordlessly, we engaged in combat. The rooftop was our arena. Blades whirled. Blows were exchanged. Every move was part of a dance of death, likely to end at any moment in a flash of steel.

Ragnark was not angry. It was almost a game for him. I think he knew what his fate was. In a heartbeat, the cold metal of his own brother's sword impaled him. For a moment, they were face to face. Ranook removed his mask. He was virtually a mirror image of

Ragnark. However, where Ragnark's face was full of character, his was hollow and devoid of emotion.

"You chose the wrong path, brother." he hissed.

"No," whispered Ragnark. "You did." and then he died. With a mighty roar, I charged Ranook. He was ready. He nimbly stepped aside and pushed me over the edge. I fell with the raindrops. This was it. This was the end of me. The rain was floating around me in suspended animation, but the rest of the world was moving all too fast. The sounds of fighting drew rapidly near.

Then, suddenly, I started slowing down. I was surrounded by little golden balls of light: *fairies*. I stopped completely only a few feet from the ground. I could feel the little fairies grabbing my clothes and tugging me upwards. Slowly, I started to rise. Faster. Faster. I was flying upwards so fast that the raindrops felt like gravel being thrown at me. The sounds of fighting died away. I rocketed past the rooftop and into the clouds, narrowly dodging a bolt of lightning. I was surrounded by fog. And then I burst out of the clouds. It was an amazing sight. The clouds fell away below me. The sky was pink from the sun. The fairies stopped and held me there for a moment. Then I was flipped head over heels back down into the clouds.

"I suppose I owe you one of the favors for that?" I said on the way down.

"No," I heard Mystique whisper. "This one's on us."

And then I was back on the roof with Ranook. "You are difficult to kill." he said calmly. I charged him. He parried my blow with ease. His blows were incredibly powerful.

I was blocking a particularly powerful one when something knocked my feet out from under me. I landed on my back. *He had tripped me.* "You cheated!" I said.

"What did you expect?" he laughed. He raised his sword for the final blow.

"No!" yelled a toddler's voice. We both turned our heads. A dragon was hovering a few feet above the roof. Jermy, Tohma, and Moguhn sat on top of the dragon's back. Tohma threw me the Bloodlust Stone. I caught it easily. "Leave him alone!" yelled Moguhn.

"No!" roared Ranook. The three toddlers hopped off the dragon.

"Morn told us to give you that." said Jermy.

"Get out of here! It's dangerous!" I yelled. It was too late. The curved blade had sliced the toddlers neatly in half. Blood sprayed everywhere.

"BASTARD!" I screamed. I hurled myself to my feet, every muscle bulging. It was part anger and part the newfound bower of the Bloodlust Stone in my spare hand. Looking back, I can barely believe what happened. I actually fought so hard that sparks flew from between the blades. And then a miracle occurred. *Somehow, I managed to drive Ranook back. He was actually afraid of me.* The blades whirled faster and faster. We nimbly leapt over bodies. Then our swords stopped. We pressed each blade against the other and brought our faces close between them.

And then I slid my foot behind his and stepped back. He fell to the roof. His sword skittered away.

"You *cheated.*" he said.

"What did you expect?" I said. I plunged my sword down. The rain became a light drizzle. A single tear slid down my cheek and fell. I went to the edge of the roof and looked away from the depressing sight.

And then something else happened. All the souls were freed. Dozens of little lights flew upwards, away from the little piles of dust that had once been their bodies. The shimmering ethereal balls of light wafted upwards on the breeze and into the clouds. There were thousands of them dancing and playing in the wind. It was one of the most amazing things I had ever seen. I smiled through my tears.

# Chapter 19
# The Return Home

Within moments I found myself on a dragon, flying back down to the ground. I landed in the midst of the Nariss, where Serrin, Morn, and Bednik were standing.

"You did it!" said Morn. "You defeated him!"

"Yes," I said. "But I did it at a price."

"What price?" Bednik said, turning pale.

"Ragnark is dead. And so are Jermy, Tohma, and Moguhn." I announced, my voice trembling.

"They shall forever be remembered as heroes." said Serrin.

"*Actually*…" hissed the Narissian king, stepping up beside us. "*You* ssshall be…forgotten. *We* will be remembered as the…heroesss."

"*What?*" yelled Serrin.

"Give…usss…the sssstone." then it dawned on me.

"*You!*" I shouted. "It was you who blew up the ship! I saw you outside the fireworks factory in Shanar before we set out! You planned this from the beginning!"

"Of courssse." he hissed. "ATTACK THEM!"

The Nariss just stood there.

"ATTACK!" he repeated. They kind of looked at each other. And then they attacked. Not us. Their king. They set upon him like wild creatures, trying to tear him from limb to limb. He was lucky enough to escape into the forest, forever banned from his own tribe.

"We did not know…that he meant…*thisss* treachery…when we…ssstole thossse fireworkssssss." explained one of the Nariss.

"Well," I said. "That explains the ship. Now who took my bag?"

"Actually," said Serrin. "I did that."

"What? Why?"

"It was just a theory." he explained hastily. "I noticed that whenever you tapped into some sort of magical force, you seemed to be tapping into the stone's power. That stone acted like a signal, giving our exact position to Ranook. I didn't want them attacking us while we were all split up like that, so I took the stone."

We spent the rest of the day remembering and laughing about our fondest memories of the people who had died that day. We bathed in the ocean that night to wash off the blood and grime.

We held five funerals the next morning. The first, Ranook, we buried simply in the ground with a wood plank as a marker.

Ragnark was burned in his coffin in a massive bonfire. The smoke twisted high into the clear air, serving as a beacon to the world about the person who had died. He would never be forgotten.

The three toddlers were buried at sea, like they would have wanted. We sailed their own homemade pirate flag and had the ship decked out with full pirate regalia. It was incredibly difficult to watch the three small coffins sink away into the sea. But a moment later, three ghostly figures flew away into the sky, laughing and playing. They weren't truly dead. Rather, they were free from all mortal worries, floating away into eternity. They would never have to worry about growing up or doing anything but playing.

From the seaport in Shanar where we buried the toddlers, we flew by dragon back to the forest, where we dropped off the Nariss. Then we flew back to Panok. We slept among the ruins of the burnt village.

The next day I said my goodbyes. Serrin led me away through the jungle, back to the Galians' tree. There he showed me a door that had been carved into the trunk of the tree. He opened it for me and I stepped inside.

"So long, friend." he said.

"See ya."

"Come back and see us sometime, all right?"

"I will." he shut the door.

The next thing I knew, I was stumbling out the air conditioning vent under my parents' bed. I finally reached my pillow. The dawn light was spreading outside the window. I was at last my normal size again. I crawled into my sleeping bag and fell asleep.

# Disclaimer

In most books, you will see a disclaimer telling you that the events of the book are fictional and come solely from the author's imagination and that any similarity between the story and real persons, living or dead, is purely coincidental. This is not quite the case with this book. The references to real people are entirely intentional. I really do live in a green van. I really do travel the United States 365 days out of the year. If you do not believe me, try visiting www.activated-storytellers.com for more information. As for the rest of the book? You decide…